# Resisting Ryann

# Resisting Ryann

USA TODAY BESTSELLER
## ALYSSA RAE TAYLOR

# 1
## Luke

I watch Gage repeatedly slap the woman in front of me. With the rest of the crew aiming their AK-47's, her tortured gaze begs me to step in. I wonder if she can see through me ... if she knows I'm not one of them. She's young, probably in her mid-twenties, possibly thirties. There are a couple of kids running around — not an ounce of fear apparent on their faces. Maybe this is a regular scene for them. Their father's gotten himself into some serious shit, and now his family is suffering the consequences. My eyes move to the five men surrounding me. If it weren't for their weapons, I could take them, but it would defeat the purpose of why I'm here, working under the thumb of my scumbag father. It's the only way to put an end to him once and for all — to keep Reese safe.

He cuts her open with the next blow. She cries out in pain as blood splatters from her lip and onto the wall. The little boy finally notices. Running to his mother's side, she tries to shoo him away, but Gage already has him in his grasp. My fingers twitch. I could reach out and snap this guy's neck, yet I do nothing. "You," he says, pointing to me. "Tie the bitch up." He shoves the trembling kid into the corner next to his sister. My gaze flicks to them before landing on the woman. There's no way I'll let that happen.

"Move!" Gage shouts, turning around to find me in the same spot.

I've never been good with orders. "She doesn't know where he is. Look at her."

"We're wasting time, boys," Marcus growls.

Gage's features darken. He ignores him and slowly steps my way. "I said, 'Tie. The. Bitch. Up.'" Each word is clearly pronounced, but I don't back down. He looks like a skinhead on crack with a face that's covered in sores. His gun is the only thing giving him confidence. I envision taking the AK and shoving it up his ass. "Think you can fool me, Romeo? I know who you are. I've been watching you a long time." He tilts his head and laughs.

"He knows we're after him. He's not going to tell her where he is." Gage takes another step, lifts the gun, and presses it against my forehead, then cocks it with shaky hands. That's when I raise mine.

"Whoa … there are kids here, man." Not that it makes a difference; he's out of his mind. A slow smirk stretches across his face.

"Gage, let's get out of here," Marcus says. Sirens play in the distance, all the while Gage is still deciding on whether or not to shoot. His agitation grows, as the woman's cries get louder. Sweating profusely, he keeps glancing her way.

"Shut up!" he yells. "Or I'll shut you up myself!" Clearly distraught, she attempts to muffle her sounds. I try to distract him by pressing harder against the end of the barrel. I'd rather him shoot me than the innocent mother in the corner.

"C'mon Gage let's go!"

I narrow my eyes, neither one of us pulling away. It's a game that we play until he presses the gun harder and violently yells, "BANG!" I flinch, and he lowers the gun, smiling proudly before making his way out the door with a wicked cackle.

My gaze moves from the boy and girl to their mother, who looks just as relieved as I am. A weak smile of gratitude appears on her face.

I search for something to say then settle for, "I'm sorry," before shutting the door and making my way toward the parking lot.

I climb into the van, and Gage tells me, "You're lucky I didn't cap your ass back there."

I give him a lethal stare and fantasize about the hundred different ways I could pummel him. We're all piled together in one vehicle, headed to meet my father. He won't be happy about the news, since we didn't get what he'd been hoping for. Gage is lucky I'm in the back. The guy brings out the worst in me.

"You can thank your daddy for that. Figured he wouldn't be happy if we came back without his pansy-ass son."

"You got a problem?" I point to the AK resting in his lap. "Lose the security blanket, and I'll help you with it."

"You know what? Blow me. Once your *dad* finally gets what's coming to him, *and he will*," he reassures, "I'm gonna find you, and I'm gonna kill you." He grins. "After I tap that little whore of yours and make you watch. How ab—"

I lunge over a row of bodies, swinging violently. Three pairs of arms attempt to hold me back. "You worthless piece of shit!" I swing harder as Gage tries to crouch underneath the dash. I push forward, wanting a piece of him. I've lost it. Behind me, the guys are shouting, pulling on my arms and legs—trying their best to keep me from murdering the prick.

"Not in the van!" Marcus yells. We all swerve to the right, then he slams his fist into Gage's side. "You trying to get us killed?

"Shit! I was messing with him!" Licking the blood from his mouth, which, fortunately for him, was the only contact I'd made. "The dude just started trippin'!" He flips down the visor, and his gaze falls on mine. The others pick up their guns, warning me to calm down. I sit back and close my eyes, rubbing the space between them. I've blocked out his words before, but this time it was different. "Don't tell me it's the whore who's got you in a tizzy. I thought you said you didn't have one?" I don't answer him; I shouldn't have reacted the way I did. As far as my father knows, Reese isn't a concern of mine anymore. My lack of sleep must finally be taking a toll on me.

"No one cares," Warren replies. The rest of the guys chuckle. "You better watch your back, Gage."

"Or what?"

"Come on. You jealous?" Marcus says with a smirk. "We got other things to worry about."

He watches me in the mirror, and a twisted grin appears on his face. I feel my jaw clench, then I press my lips into a tight line and fold my arms, resting my head against the back of the seat. It's too tempting to stare him down, so I close my eyes and try to clear my mind. The bastard isn't worth my time.

He snickers as though he can read what I'm thinking. "Believe me, Ryann ... the feeling's mutual."

We pull up to an abandoned warehouse, never meeting my father in the same place, therefore lessening our chances of getting caught. Like always, I'm the last to know the location. Nobody trusts me at this point, but that's smart. They shouldn't. One by one we climb out of the van and make our way around the back. My father and the rest of his entourage are already here. There's a woman standing by his side, maybe a hooker. All I know is that I've never seen her before, and she can't be much older than

Reese.

"You're late," my father says. His two overweight bodyguards step forward. I raise my arms, and they pat me down, checking to see if I'm wired. It's an occurrence I've become accustomed to.

"You can blame your son for that," Gage replies, tipping his head in my direction. Man, I'd love to knock whatever's left of his teeth down his throat.

"Luke?"

I respond to my father, "We couldn't find him."

"And his wife?"

"We tried. She said she didn't know anything, and I believe her. Then dipshit over here got a hard-on and wouldn't leave her alone." I glance at Gage. "It took some convincing for him to finally realize the feelings weren't mutual."

My father purses his lips, while the rest of the guys laugh. Gage raises his gun. "You lying sack of ..."

"Put it down, Gage. There's no need for violence," my father says calmly before his eyes flick to mine. "You two need to start figuring out how to get along," he says, pointing between us, "or things are going to get messy." Gage scowls, and I drop my gaze to the floor. "Samuel owes me a lot of money. We don't have time for this crap; you need to find him. Understand?"

We look at each other and nod, neither of us meaning it. Pretending to be my father's puppet takes practice. While most of them have it down, I'm still getting the hang of it. Every guy is in this for himself. If getting along with Gage will earn me a gun, then that's what I'll do. You can't trust anyone in this business, and I can only do so much using my bare hands.

"So what's the plan, boys? The clock is ticking." He looks at his watch.

"We go back, get the wife and kids. Kill 'em off one by one. If he cares about his family, he won't have a choice but to give us the money." Gage grins, and that's when I snap.

"Are you really that hard up? 'Cause if you're looking to get off, I can think of several other options. A couple of them being a willing participant and your hand."

Gage strides toward me. "I've had enough of your mouth, damn it! I could have ended you back at the apartment." He turns to my father, pleading, "You said he was dead to you. How about I make it official and put us all out of our misery?" Marcus and Warren hold him back. I stay where I am, craving the confrontation. Let him come.

My father tilts his head, and I see the evil lurking behind his eyes. "Do you know who my son is, Gage?" he asks. I groan under my breath. I don't want him turning this into a show. These are people's lives that we're messing with. When Gage doesn't respond, he says, "Tell him, son."

I raise a brow, hesitating, not wanting to go there. "Nah, it's all right." I put my hands in my pockets, rocking back on my heels. "How about we go home, get some shut-eye? Pick up where we left off in the morning?" It's late, and I'm tired.

He makes his way over, places his hand on my back, and leans in. His breath sweeps across my face. "Humble isn't a good look on you, son." He turns around. "Would someone do me the honors of filling Gage in? Surely one of you knows."

"I don't care who he is," Gage grumbles, his fists clenched closely at his sides.

"Let it go, Dad." The word slips out of my mouth before I can take it back—call it an error in judgment due to sleep deprivation. I haven't called him that in ages, and I don't plan on starting now.

"He's a professional fighter. Mixed martial arts," Warren tells him. "I told you, Gage, you're playing with fire."

"Again, I don't care who he is."

"Marcus, take his gun."

I narrow my eyes as Marcus obeys. You're kidding me. "You want me to fight him?"

He smiles. "I do. In fact, I'm looking forward to it." The rest of the guys egg us on, already pumped to see some action. Gage just stares me down, bobbing his head as though he's ready to start.

I let out a laugh. "Trust me. I'd love to give this dick what he deserves, but I won't go easy on him — not after what he pulled today." I stare back.

"Who said anything about easy?"

Gage bounces around, circling his shoulders, then spits. "You don't scare me, asshole." Wiping his mouth with the back of his hand, Gage all but begs for me to fight him … and I will. That piece of shit preys on defenseless women and wouldn't think twice about taking the life of a child. Today's memory brings a spike of adrenaline that now overshadows my fatigue. Suddenly, slamming my fist through his teeth no longer seems like such a bad idea.

I rotate my wrists, stretching out my neck and shoulders. "You sure you want to do this?"

Pulling his shirt over his head and tossing it behind him, he says, "Never been more sure of anything in my life."

# 2

## Reese

I lie awake, frozen at the sound of someone walking outside my bedroom window, a shadow lurking on the wall. My father left me with tearstained cheeks, the taste still lingering on my tongue. I wipe them away and climb out of bed, searching my room for a weapon. I'd rather do this alone than involve the person responsible for the throbbing above my eye. Reaching for my bat, I creep toward the window, hoping my imagination has gotten the best of me. The only barrier I have is the thin cotton material of my curtain. An outline of a person stands on the other side. My pulse quickens, and my body trembles. I'm terrified. Stretching out the bat, using the end to open the curtain, I find a boy holding up his hands. He takes a step back.

"I didn't mean to scare you." His gaze is steady on the bat. "You're safe. I promise," he says, his voice calm.

I loosen my grip, recognizing the boy from across the street, then place my weapon on the ground, embarrassed. I don't know why he's here. He's older—he drives a car—and we've barely ever talked to each other.

The darkness outside makes my injury easier to hide. Maybe he won't notice. He watches me with gentle eyes, and the corner of his mouth tips up.

*I look at what he's wearing, assuming he just crawled out of bed. He's got on pajama pants and a hoodie that doesn't match. His hair is sticking up. It's the middle of January. It's cold, late—too late for him to be here—and way past my bedtime. If my father catches us, I'll be hiding my face for a while.*

*Realizing that my weapon is no longer a threat, he lowers his hands.* "Can you hear me? I'll try to be quiet."

*I peek over my shoulder to check that my door is still closed; I turn and give him a nod.*

"You probably shouldn't talk," *he replies.* "I don't want you to get into trouble." *When I look at him, confused, he adds,* "Just nod your head yes or no. All right?"

*I agree.*

*His gaze falls to the ground, and he scratches the back of his head.* "I saw what happened … with your dad earlier." *Shoving his hands into his pockets, he continues,* "Are you hurt?" *he asks sincerely.*

*I want to disappear. He saw my dad hit me? I blush. Probably saw me crying, too. Closing my eyes, mortified, I wonder what all he had seen, and how it looked from the outside.*

"Does he do it a lot?"

*My eyes open. I press my lips into a tight line and force myself to answer. It's only when he drinks. If it weren't for the alcohol, he wouldn't do it. The problem, though? He drinks all the time.*

*His gaze stays on mine.* "You know it's wrong, right?" *He cocks a brow.*

*Of course I know it's wrong. I nod.*

"Have you told anyone?"

*Only you. I shake my head, and he gestures toward his house.*

"Come find me if he does it again." *He lifts his chin.* "I'll teach him a lesson."

*The thought of him teaching my father a lesson makes me laugh. It's nice of him to offer, but he obviously doesn't know how strong he is.*

*"What?" He gives me a dimpled grin. "You don't think I could take him?"*

*Shaking my head, I smile but try to hide it.*

*His eyes widen. "Shit! Is that blood?"*

*I flinch, touching the spot where my face had hit the dresser. Pulling back a sticky piece of hair, I meet his eyes, and his expression goes hard.*

*He reaches for my chin. "I'm not going to hurt you," he whispers, turning it toward him, carefully eyeing the injury. "That's going to leave a scar." I don't know what to say, so I stay quiet while he examines the rest of my face. "I could kill him," he hisses, releasing me and looking around. "I better go," he points. "You should get back in bed. I don't want to risk you getting in trouble again."*

*I nod.*

*"Don't forget what I said." He lifts his brows, walking backward toward his house, nearly tripping when he almost misses the curb. It makes me smile.*

My eyes pop open, and I'm short of breath. The ceiling fan spins above me. How am I supposed to move past this when my memories constantly bring him back? My chest tightens as the familiar ache burns from deep within, triggering tears I don't want to cry anymore. I hate him—hate him for what he's done to me. I grab a pillow and throw it against the wall. I doubt I'll be getting any sleep tonight.

"**G**et off of me, Logan! It isn't funny," I growl, jabbing my elbows into his chest. He chuckles, taking his time before slowly rolling away, finding my effort amusing. The man drives me crazy. If he weren't my best friend's boyfriend, I'd take the opportunity to knee him in the balls. It's a fantasy I have on a regular basis.

"Why are you always laughing at me?" I brush off my shorts. He had me pinned face down on the ground. It isn't the first time, and I doubt it will be the last. Like Luke, he pushes my buttons, except he takes it to a completely different level that I didn't know was possible.

He quickly stands. "I like to find the humor in things," he says, leaning against the counter, crossing his feet at his ankles. "You should try it." Then he strikes a pose to show off his muscles. I realize what he's doing when an attractive woman walks by and shoots him a flirty look. He eats it up, his ego growing by the second. She's wearing boy shorts that expose three-quarters of her butt. He purses his lips, and his eyes follow the back of her as she walks farther away.

"Maybe if you look long enough, you'll get to see her vagina."

He grins. "I hope so," he says, keeping his gaze on her backside until she's completely out of view. He's messing with me; it's what he likes to do.

"Earlier ... you were saying?"

I'm about ready to tell him when he interrupts, "Oh yeah, something about my sense of humor, and your lack of one."

I glare. "You repeatedly pinning me to the ground isn't humorous. It's annoying," I say, reaching back to smooth out the mess that is my hair.

His eyes crinkle at the sides. "You know you secretly like it."

"You're a pig."

He fakes a frown. "There's no need for name calling, little virgin. I do it to prepare you, and I promised a buddy I'd cover what he hadn't. Whether you like it or not is irrelevant."

I roll my eyes. "What is it that Gia sees in you? Did your

mother ever teach you any manners—perhaps the meaning of the word *no*?"

"You know this is different." Walking behind the counter, he opens up a drawer and pulls out a protein bar. "I already told you," he says as he takes a bite. "I made a promise ... and I'm gon—"

"It doesn't matter what you promised."

He stops chewing. "How so?"

"Because, I've moved on, and so should you." That's not entirely true, but I'm trying.

Logan took Luke's place here at work, which apparently was another promise I was left unaware of until the day he walked in, strutting around the gym as if he owned it. Luke prepared Jim and Pam in advance, and Logan agreed to take over. I guess it worked out for all of them. Logan dating my best friend is hard enough, but having to work with him ... well, it's nearly unbearable.

"You trying to convince me or yourself?"

"You read the letter." I blow out a breath. "Forget it. I don't want to get into this again."

It's been five months. I haven't heard from Luke in the last three, and only a handful of times before that. It started with a few texts I received from an unknown number, saying things like, "I miss you," or, "When this is all over, I'll explain everything," and finally followed by, "Do you trust me?" I never replied to any of them, though a few times I came close.

Why the untraceable number? I didn't know, but I definitely didn't like it. The last one came around three months ago. Telling me he loved me—that it killed him to be away from me. I read it at least a hundred times, wanting to believe he had good reason for all of this. I needed to know the truth, and he wasn't planning to give it … at least not anytime soon.

One day I received a package with no return address. When I opened it, I found a Taser gun wrapped in a bow with a note that read: KEEP THIS ON YOU. ASK LOGAN TO SHOW YOU HOW TO USE IT. IT'S IMPORTANT.

*What the hell?*

"Forget about the letter," he groans. "He didn't mean it." He waves goodbye to one of our regulars, and I do the same.

"How am I supposed to forget it? I can't."

He shrugs. "Maybe I have more faith in him than you do." Finishing what's left in his mouth, he throws the wrapper in the trash.

"Faith has nothing to do with it. He wrote it, Logan."

The letter said he was sorry for all that he had done, that he would always love me, but it was best we *both* move on. He wanted me to be happy … blah blah blah … and a person like him doesn't deserve a person like me. It was the last time I'd heard from him. He had made his point pretty clear.

"Doesn't matter." He folds his arms. "There are things I know about him that you don't. And you *won't* until it's over. Things aren't always what they seem. Remember that."

"Don't worry, I will."

"Do you miss him?"

The question catches me off guard. "I don't want to," I reply.

He grins with a nod. "Good." *Jerk.*

"Are you one of those people who secretly gets off on torturing animals?" I narrow my eyes.

"Nope." He guzzles down a full bottle of water, then crushes the plastic.

"I'm not sure I believe you."

"Believe what you want." Glancing at the clock, I see there are only ten minutes left before his class starts. "You leaving?"

"Yeah, I just need to get my stuff." I head to the counter, and he walks behind it.

"Do me a favor," he says, grabbing my purse. "Tell Gia to wear the *red one* tonight." He hands it over. "She'll know what it means."

*Eww.* "You couldn't just tell her that yourself?"

His mouth tips up. "Thought it'd be more fun to have you do it instead."

"I guess that's my queue." I turn around and wave. "See ya."

"You planning to see *loverboy* again?" he asks from behind me.

I glance at him suspiciously. "Maybe … why?"

He shrugs. "You may need to defend yourself from *him* one day, and I'd be happy to help you with that. Just let me know."

"Oh, I'm sure you would. Look … Sean's been a good friend to me, but nothing more. Be nice, okay?"

He snorts. "Right." He emphasizes the word. "A friend who'd love to get inside your panties."

"Not all men are like you," I retort, pushing past the door. "Good bye," I yell.

"If you can't see that this guy's a bigger douche than *I* am, then you're blind," he yells back. I do my best to ignore him and crawl inside my car.

Sean's and my friendship sparked at a time when I needed someone most. If I wasn't drowning myself in work, I was spending much of my days alone. If that wasn't possible, I was forced to be around Logan and Gia's constant display of affection. Their relationship had blossomed, while mine had fallen apart. After months of making excuses for him, becoming everything I never wanted to be, I'd finally had enough. I'd climbed up to the rooftop to get some air. I'd only been there a minute when a familiar male voice called out to me. I peeked over the edge. Sean stood below, looking nervous as he stared up at me. I could see that he was carefully choosing his words.

*"You expecting company?"*

*I contemplate turning him away like I've done before. Instead I reply, "No."*

*He lifts his brows, clearly surprised. "Would you mind some?"*

*"I don't know," I reply, regretting it. "I mean, yes, I'd like some, sorry." I close my eyes, embarrassed. When I open them, he is already climbing up, and he is smiling — probably laughing at me. I would, too, if I was him. I am a mess.*

*"So you finally said yes," he murmurs. "What made you change your mind?"*

*I lie down on the blanket and focus on the stars. "Believe me, I was doing you a favor. I haven't been that much fun these last few months."*

*"You going to tell me why you're so sad all the time?" Sitting down beside me, he leaves plenty of space between us so it won't be awkward. My gaze moves over to him, and he taps a spot on his shoulder. "I'll let you borrow these to cry on if you need to." He shrugs. "Won't bother me any."*

*I grin, which is something I haven't done in a while. I hold out a hand, saying, "To be honest ... I think I could really use a friend."*

*Watching me cautiously before he takes, he smiles. "If you let me, I think I could be that friend."*

*We shake on it. "Good," I nodded. "Then it's settled."*

# 3

## Luke

"My money's on Ryann," Marcus says.

Gage scowls in his direction. "You want to go next?"

Marcus is in his face, "That a promise?"

"Let's do this," I tell them, sick and tired of their banter.

Gage shoots me a twisted grin, charging toward me like a mad man. I guess he's ready to start. "Show me what you got," he says, swinging erratically. I almost feel sorry for him when I slam a fist into his pancreas. Then the other one hits his jaw. He staggers back, using the car parked behind him for leverage. He spits out a mouthful of blood, and I give him a minute to clear his head before signaling him to come closer. He takes the bait, pushing toward me, and puts all his energy into his swing, only landing a few body shots. It hurts, but not enough to do damage. He's frustrated and tired.

Using my knee as a ploy, I strike him, and he blocks me. I thank him by sending an uppercut straight to his chin, following through with a left hook. He stumbles to the ground, walking backward on his hands. I let him up. He dives right at me, wrapping his arms around my waist—a weak attempt to take me down. I pound the side of his head over and over. He's on his way down again. Everyone's shouting, his earlier words replaying in my head. I stare at his broken face. He slowly comes to a stand. I'm amazed he's still conscious.

"Is that all you got?"

"You sure you want more?" My mouth curves into a grin. The dude doesn't quit. It's impressive.

He spits. "You ain't seen nothin' yet, mother fucker."

I go with a different approach, taking him to the ground. It may be my weakness, but this guy isn't a threat to me, and I'm tired of watching his crazy ass get up. I want to end this now. He rolls onto his side, scooting away, but not really going anywhere. I reach around his neck and easily put him in a chokehold. He grips my forearm with both of his hands, squeezing and pulling, trying to loosen my hold, but there isn't any use. I've got him locked in securely. This is over. "Tap out," I tell him. "It's all you've got to do."

He continues to struggle. "Fuck you," he chokes out, his air supply close to non-existent. The son of a bitch won't give up, even knowing he doesn't have a chance. I think he'd rather pass out.

I squeeze tighter. "Tap, dude. You're going out."

He removes a hand from my arm and slowly presses it to the concrete. He's ready to tap. He's turning blue.

"You giving up?"

He taps.

I want to make sure he means it. "Is that a yes?"

His legs are shaking, and he taps again, making it obvious for everyone to see. There's no question he's tapping out. I let him go, and he gasps before spitting out another mouthful of blood. He rolls onto his back, throwing an arm over his eyes. I grab my shirt, wipe off the sweat and blood, then toss it over my shoulder.

I walk away without looking back. I'm done.

"You just got your ass handed to you, Gage," Marcus cackles. Glancing at my father and his female friend, he waves me over. There's a gleam in his eye.

"I almost forgot … have the two of you been introduced?" He gestures between us. My eyes move to the petite brunette by his side. She eyes me curiously, like she knows something I don't. "I'll take that as a, 'No,'" he answers. "Rachelle, this is Luke, my son, as I've already told you. Luke, this is Rachelle," he appraises her. "Rachelle and I are *close*. I've been meaning to introduce you for some time."

Reaching out her hand, I ignore it. "So, this is Luke," she quips, her sultry voice sending a message. "I've heard so much about you." If she stood any closer, we'd be touching.

"Likewise," I reply, uninterested in her advances. I didn't come here to make friends. Glancing at my father, I say, "I'm out."

"What? You're not going to fight anymore?" Rachelle asks, placing a hand on my chest and surprising me when her eyes lift to mine. "Winner takes all?"

"Not tonight." I step back, slowly removing her hand. "This wasn't for you, cupcake."

"I never said it was." She lifts her chin defiantly. Good, I've offended her.

My father smirks beside her. "Tomorrow maybe," he joins, not minding that his *close friend* wants to test-drive the younger Ryann. Why would he bring her?

"Luke, you coming?" Marcus shouts.

I look over my shoulder and raise a finger. "Hold up."

Back to my father. "Why's she here?" I ask, tipping my head toward Rachelle. "What is this?"

His grin is menacing. He leans forward and pats me on the back. "If you want me to share son, just ask."

Real smooth. "Cut the bullshit. You know this isn't a place for her," I spit. "If something goes wrong, they'll take her." Meaning the cartel. "She'll be used as a sex slave the rest of her life. It's a stupid move, and you know it."

He stiffens. "Rachelle being here isn't up to you. And *you*, my son, better not forget who you're talking to."

"Then who's it up to? And don't worry, I haven't." I glance at Rachelle, who's in shock. "Are you scared? Cause you should be."

"I … uh," she stutters. I've put her on the spot.

"How old are you … low-to-mid twenties?" I ask.

By her expression, you'd think I'd wanted the color of her panties. "I'm twenty-five." She's a year younger than me.

I raise my brows. "You want to make it to your next birthday?"

Gazing at my father, she says, "Of course. What's *that* supposed to mean?"

"It *means*, if you walk away now, you *might* have a chance."

He interrupts, "Rachelle is capable of making her own decisions. Luke is just toying with you my, dear."

My fingers ache to hit him. "Capable." I nod. "Like Mom … you mean?"

"Yes," he clips, working the tension in his jaw. "Just like your mom."

Reese

"Hanging out with Beckham tonight?" Gia asks, startling me. I just stepped out of the shower. She's lying on my bed, gazing up at the ceiling. Beckham is the nickname she gave Sean the first day she met him. He earned it because of his striking resemblance to the soccer player … well, minus the tattoos.

"You nearly gave me a heart attack," I reply, short of breath, placing a hand over my heart. "Yes, I am, but I needed to shower first. I felt gross."

"Sorry," she murmurs. "Not because you feel gross, or because of Beckham, but for the near heart attack," she reassures. "I didn't mean to scare you."

I slip on some jeans and a V-neck before making my way to the bed. Judging by her expression, I can easily tell that something is bothering her. "What?"

She arches a brow, feigning innocence. "What do you mean?" I've seen the look many times. We've known each other since elementary school. It's hard to get anything past one another.

"I know that face. What's going on?"

"Is it that obvious?" She fidgets with her necklace.

I nod.

Releasing a breath, she says, "Fine … Logan texted me."

I roll my eyes. "Why'd I even ask?"

"He said you were going to come home and *talk shit*," she quotes. "He didn't have time to explain, but told me I'd get it from you. I'm almost afraid to ask. What'd he do?"

"I don't want to talk about it right now. It's exhausting, and I'm not in the mood to argue. Later."

"Wait a minute," she replies. "What makes you think I would argue? Is this something about me?" her voice squeaks.

"No, not at all." I hold out my hands. "I promise. The words just didn't come out the way I meant." I sigh, and she scoots over, so I lie next to her. "Logan was giving me crap about Sean. It's hard when he brings up the *L* word. You know?" I look at her. "He has this way of making me feel guilty … like I'm doing something wrong."

She furrows her brows. "I had a feeling that's what this was about. I'm sorry, Reese," she murmurs. "I'm not sure why he has a problem with Sean. When I brought him up the other day he freaked out."

"What happened?"

"I told him I was glad you seemed better. At first, he agreed. But, as soon as I mentioned Sean being the reason, he got all caveman and started accusing me of having a *thing* for *the neighbor*," she snorts. "So I dropped it."

"Insecure much?"

"Tell me about it." We both laugh. "What'd he say to you?"

Not wanting to cause any more drama, I say, "It doesn't really matter anymore. I'm over it."

"Yes, it does. Tell me," she nudges. "You can't leave here until you do. I'll lock you in. I swear."

I roll my eyes. "He doesn't believe Luke meant what he said

in the letter. He thinks it'll all makes sense when he comes back, and I'll understand why he did it."

She chews on her lip. "He's told me the same thing."

"And?"

"And?"

"Do you believe him?" A big part of me wants her to tell me she does.

"I don't know," she sighs. "I'm pissed he left you here without any answers. And I just can't think of a good enough excuse for you to be okay with that."

I groan. "I feel the same way." I sit up, and she does the same, putting an arm around my shoulders.

"What did he say about Sean?"

I grin because he's predictable. "That he's a douche ... and he just wants to get inside my panties."

She rolls her eyes, giggling. "Typical Logan," she says, shaking her head. "What an ass! First of all, what *straight guy* wouldn't want to crawl inside of a woman's panties? It's human nature." She shrugs. "Has he tried anything since the first time?"

"No." Sean went in for a kiss near the beginning. I acted as if he was attempting to take my virginity—spitting out a million excuses as to why I wasn't ready. By the end of the night, I realized I had rambled on for hours. Other than *goodbye*, I never even gave him a chance to reply. Yep ... something is truly wrong with me.

"See? Doesn't sound like a douche to me, and let's not forget who he looks like ... David Beckham," she replies enthusiastically.

"I'm not sure his good looks will earn him any points with Logan. If anything, it'll work against him. Caveman, remember?"

She pauses. "Okay, maybe you're right. Let me tell you. It helps him with me," Gia quips, wiggling her brows. "And I just came up with a brilliant idea that *may* solve our little problem."

"You're breaking up with Logan," I joke, hopping off the bed. I know she wouldn't do that. She loves him too much, and I wouldn't want that for her.

"No, no. Not that." She looks off in the distance. "Dinner." Slowly, she nods. "The four of us, here. We'll force them to become friends." She lights up like it's the best idea she's ever had.

I shake my head. "No way. I refuse to do that to Sean."

She frowns. "Come on. It's the only way. Think about it."

"I am. Logan sees him as a threat." I run a comb through my hair and throw it up in a bun. "Nothing will ever change that as long as his loyalty stands with Luke. It doesn't matter that Sean and I are just friends."

"In normal circumstances I'd agree, but not if I threaten to take his privileges away … like in the *bedroom*," she says suggestively, raising her brows.

Logan would hate to have his bedroom privileges taken away. "You may have a point." I tilt my head. "Huh, okay … I'll think about it."

Her face stretches into a huge smile. "Awesome!"

"**A**re you anxious to see me, or were you just being hospitable?" I didn't even have a chance to knock.

He gives me a wide grin, smelling like he's freshly showered. "Both," he replies, reaching in for a hug. I step out of it quicker than I normally would, feeling a twinge of guilt. He frowns. "Everything okay?"

"Yeah, I'm fine." I smile, not wanting to explain any further. None of this is his fault. I walk around him. "Just had a long day." I make my way to the lazy boy chair. I'm reminded of how different Sean is from the stereotypical bachelor. He's clean, almost to a fault. There's something about a man who keeps his things in order. I glance at the stacks of files spread across the dining table. "Working on a case?"

"I was," Sean says, gathering up his work and setting it aside. He eyes me

suspiciously. "Sure you're okay?"

Gee, am I that obvious? I grin. "I already told you. I'm fine." Fidgeting with my shirt, I successfully avoid his eyes. "Are all those for one case?" I ask, pointing to the mess.

He looks over. "I've got a handful that I'm working on." Sean's a prosecuting attorney. He spends most of his days researching and rarely discusses his work. I guess it's a confidentiality thing — either that, or he'd rather keep his work separate from his personal life. "You want a beer?" he asks, striding toward the fridge. He's only being considerate.

"A water sounds perfect," I sigh, not comfortable drinking around him. I've learned through past experience, the combination of alcohol and men make my inhibitions non-existent.

"What's going on in that head of yours?" he asks, handing me the water. "You seem distracted." He takes a pull from his bottle. I hadn't noticed the long-sleeve button-down, fashionable jeans, and *new* leather shoes he's sporting.

"I like your shoes," I tell him, giving him a once-over. "You look nice. Why are you all dressed up?" Silently, I'm hoping it isn't for me.

"I thought I'd get you out of the house for a change." He shrugs, taking another swig. "But judging by your face, I'm guessing you want to stay in tonight."

"What's wrong with my face?"

He chuckles. "I didn't say anything was wrong with it. You just look upset. That's all." He makes his way to the couch and flips on the television. "You going to sit way over there all night? We still need to catch up on *The Walking Dead*."

I can't believe I'm being this way. Logan shouldn't have a say in what I do or whom I do it with. I go to the spot beside him, taking a seat. "I wanted to ask you something."

"Now we're getting somewhere." He grins, setting his beer on the coffee table. Stretching his arms behind his neck, he leans against the couch. "Ask away."

"Do you work late tomorrow?"

His eyes roam to the stack of files in the corner. "Depends. Did you want to go out?"

"No. Not exactly, but you're close." Closing one eye, I'm afraid of his response. He may be polite to Logan's face, but I know he doesn't care for him. "I was wondering if you'd like to come over for dinner — my place this time."

"I'd love to," he replies before I'm finished.

Now for the hard part. "We thought it'd be a good idea for the four of us to get together."

He tilts his head.

"Gia and I, I mean."

I watch his face fall, but he recovers quickly. The corner of his mouth tips up. "Give me the time, and I'll be there."

"Really?"

He looks at me, surprised. "Of course, why wouldn't I?"

"Cause Logan can be a real jerk," I murmur.

"He seems like an all right guy." He shrugs, taking his empty bottle to the trash, before grabbing another. "Now I want to ask you something."

"Uh oh."

"Don't be scared." He smiles as he strides back over. "If I go tomorrow, will you let me take you out this weekend?" He sits down. "As friends. I promise I won't try to kiss you." I cover my face, embarrassed. "Unless, of course, you want me to," he adds.

I peek through my fingers. "I'm not scared, and I trust you. To be honest, I could use a little getting out of the house."

"I agree." He lifts his bottle. So I grab my glass of water. We clink them together. "I have a feeling things are going to get interesting." We both take a sip.

"What do you mean?" I ask.

Letting out a sharp laugh, he licks his lips. "To tell you the truth ... I don't know." He kicks his feet up on the table. "It's just a feeling." It doesn't take long before the both of us become engrossed in the zombies on the screen.

W ill's voice startles me awake, along with a woman's I don't recognize. I must have fallen asleep during one of the episodes. I had made it through at least three. Now I'm sprawled out on the couch and have no idea where Sean went.

"Ah man, did we wake you?" Will asks, glancing around. Although Will and Sean are roommates, I rarely see him. It seems like he's never home.

I yawn. "Yeah, it's fine." Gazing down the hall, I look for Sean. "Sean must be in the bathroom. Will you tell him I went home? And sorry I fell asleep on him?" As soon as the words leave my mouth, he enters the room.

"Enjoy your nap?" He smiles.

"Told you it was a long day. I'm going home now. I need to sleep."

"You want me to walk you?"

"No, I'll be fine." I reach over and give him a hug, then introduce myself to Will's friend, since Will so rudely forgot. I turn around to Sean. "Dinner tomorrow," I point. "When I figure out more details, I'll call or text."

He nods. "I'll be there. Sleep tight."

"I'll try." I shut the door and make my way home, anticipating a night of dreamless sleep.

# 5
## Luke

I've taken my fourth shower of the day trying to wash the filth away. It's imprinted on my skin like a jagged scar. These past few months have been haunting my conscience. Who would have thought I'd be back in the middle of the cesspool I'd fought so hard to stay away from? I guess that's the way life goes. You get what you're given. Shut up and deal with the consequences.

I search for my only source of communication that'll get me through the day. I need to talk to Andrew. *Where are you, little bastard?* Reaching into the vent, I feel around for the phone. I must've pushed it farther back the last time I used it. I stand on my toes and am able to grab it, then quickly dial the number. He answers on the first ring, which is usual for him, though he never knows when to expect me.

"You all right?"

I take a glance at the clock. "Peachy. Look, I don't have much time."

"I understand," he murmurs. "Talk to me."

"It's Valdez. We're meeting in twenty minutes." I pinch the bridge of my nose.

"You serious?" he asks, hopeful. It's the opportunity both of us have been waiting for.

"Serious as a heart attack."

"You get a location?"

No, dipshit. "I told you. They don't give me that information." I rake my hand through my hair and pace back and forth. "Can they put a tail on me?" I place the phone on speaker and finish getting dressed.

"Nah, too risky. Either way, it means we're close. What do you got on him?"

"One of our guys screwed up a coke deal — took off with over half a mil. I'm headed down to clean up the mess ... smooth things over." I lick my lips. "I hadn't heard about Valdez's involvement until today. Called you as soon as I found out."

"You know what this means," he says. "If all goes well, you could be getting out of there within a few days." I grin at his words, though I find it unlikely. "What's that idiot thinking, taking off with the money?"

No idea. "All I know is his wife and kids are suffering for it."

He clears his throat. "I'm sorry to hear that."

"Yeah, so am I." I picture the terror on each of their faces. "So what's next after this?"

Sighing into the phone, he says, "The deal has to go through. It's very important you make it happen, Luke."

I blow out a breath. "And if it doesn't?"

"Then the feds won't make their move, and you'll be stuck there a little longer. They need the evidence. It's the only way to convict him."

I'm ready to throw the phone against the wall and shatter it into a million pieces. I have no authority here. We're dealing with a drug-lord who makes my father's cruelest of crimes look like Mother Theresa's. "That's the best they can do?" I peek out the window. "You're serious?" I growl, sitting down on the bed.

"Listen."

"No, you listen. This was supposed to be about Reese—about putting my father in prison so she would be safe. Now I'm wondering if this was a mistake!" I tighten my grip on the phone.

"Look," he says calmly. "You didn't have a choice. I know this is hard for you. Just hang in there, and we'll get him."

I snort. "Easy for you to say."

"This is hard for me, too. Do you realize how much praying I've been doing? Let me tell you. *A lot.* It'd do *you* good to give it a try," he murmurs.

"Thanks for the advice, but I'm pretty sure Jesus isn't going to help me with this one."

He laughs. "If He helped me. He sure as hell wouldn't have a problem helping you."

A car pulls up the drive. "Yeah, where is he then? Look, I got to go. Tell the feds thanks for nothing"

Andrew mumbles something back, but I end the call and put the phone away, then head out to the car where Marcus and Warren are waiting.

We're in the middle of the desert. I've seen nothing but dirt, cactus, and tumbleweeds for the past forty minutes. Although I'm curious where Gage is, I don't ask, assuming he's licking his wounds at home—still weak from the beat down I gave him. I'm glad I don't have to deal with him today.

We finally spot a couple SUVs and a van parked off in the distance. Marcus heads that way, then we pull over to park the car. I count six of them, opposed to our three, as we all climb out of our vehicles. All of them are visibly armed, except for a middle-aged man wearing a suit with his hair greased back. I assume this is Valdez.

He steps forward and reaches out a hand. "Gentlemen."

Marcus and Warren give their formal hellos, but Valdez keeps his gaze on mine. "Luke Ryann," he says with a fake smile. "I've watched you fight. I've got to say, I'm a big fan." His eyes tell me the opposite. I use my game face pretending I didn't notice the animosity in his voice. He's my one-way ticket to Reese's safety. Once the feds get what they want, my father is no longer a threat, then Reese and I can get on with our lives. I just hope she'll be able to forgive me and understand I did what I had to do.

"I appreciate that, sir."

His eyebrows pinch together. "I'm curious, though, what brings you to the business?" he asks, lifting his chin. His men all stand behind him.

I scan each one of them, noticing most of their sizes evenly match mine, and I'm a big guy. "Just keeping it in the family, sir." My eyes flick back to him.

He rubs his chin. "I thought you might say that." He takes a couple steps back. "Your father and I have done business for years."

"So I've heard."

He lets out a short laugh. "Really? I'm surprised by that." There's a bite in his tone. "Tell me, what else have you heard?" Lifting his brows, he watches my expression.

"I wish I had more to give you, but my father keeps the details of his business practices private." I keep my face blank.

He nods, seeming pleased by my answer. "It's too bad our meeting isn't under better circumstances," he adds, giving me a firm pat on the shoulder.

"I agree, but we can't let it slow us down, right?"

"No, we can't," he replies.

I gesture to Marcus and Warren. "You guys go ahead." Valdez looks amused by this. I hold out my hands. "Like I said, I don't get much of the details. These guys are who you want to talk to."

He smirks. "I guess you're going to have to earn back your father's trust. Am I right?"

I tense at his words then quickly release it. *How the hell does he know?* "I guess so," I tell him, meeting his eyes. A whole lot of scenarios run through my mind—about my past, and his possible involvement—but it's not the time to be distracted by that.

"We still want the deal," Marcus tells him. "It just may take a little longer to get the money. There are a few more leads we need to follow. Some of our guys are on it now. Could be later today, tomorrow … three days tops."

"You sound pretty confident you'll catch him," Valdez replies with his hands clasped behind his back. "What happens if you don't?"

"You'll get the money regardless," Warren answers. "There are other sources we can use if we have to."

"Good. Then I don't see a problem moving forward."

"We're glad to hear that," Warren replies with an easy grin. He lifts his brows. "You bring us a sample?"

Valdez looks over his shoulder. "Salinas," he calls.

A dude with a buzz cut and a full sleeve of tattoos heads over to the van then opens it. *Holy shit!* I blink, hoping it's a hallucination from my lack of sleep. We make our way to the gruesome scene. A lump forms in the pit of my stomach, and my jaw clenches tightly.

"Where's the dog?" one of the men say from behind me.

"I stopped to take a piss. He attacked the fuck out of me and got away," another one retorts.

"You shoot it?"

"I said I was taking a piss. He ran off."

"Told you the dog was a bad idea. Dumb ass."

I block out their voices, flicking my gaze to Marcus and Warren, finding their only focus is the coke. Neither one of them sparing a glance at the decapitated bodies, or the young girl that's gagged and bound between them. She's very much alive, petrified, with tears streaming down her cheeks. She can't be much older than thirteen.

Flies swarm the headless corpses, and bile creeps up my throat.

"Are those her parents?"

"Not anymore," Salinas replies, brushing the hair away from her face.

She cringes from his touch.

A suggestive smile plays on his lips. "Pretty, isn't she?" he asks.

I clench my fists, conflicted. "Sure." I swallow, knowing her future doesn't look so good. She'll be lucky if she isn't raped, sold, or murdered like her parents. "What do you plan to do with her?"

"What do you think?" He tips his head toward the bodies. "She's the spitting image of her mother." He smirks. "She's going to make us some Benjamins."

My fist slams into his mouth a moment later, and he falls to the ground, lying unconscious on his back. I guess I snapped without even a thought.

"Enough, Luke!" I hear Warren shout, holding me back with the help of Marcus.

It takes a total of three seconds to notice Valdez's men are circled around me, their weapons pointed at my face.

"Put them down," Valdez orders. They do as they're told. I lower my hands, and he makes his way toward me. "So you have a soft spot for children," he says when he's close.

I squeeze my eyes shut, then open them. "I'm sorry, sir." I might have ruined everything in that moment.

He pulls a gun from his jacket. "I never liked Salinas," he says, shooting him in the head like he means nothing to him. His blood drains into the dirt. My pulse picks up. I do what I can to stay calm.

Putting the gun away, he pats me on the shoulder. "You didn't come here to discuss the girl. Did you, Mr. Ryann?" he asks, raising his brows.

I meet his seedy eyes. "No, sir." But I'll get her away from you if I can.

He tilts his head. "Do you know what happens if you betray me?"

I nod. "I think I have a good idea."

He watches me, then paces back and forth, like he's thinking. He stops. "I consider your father a friend," he says, pursing his lips. "This is your only warning." He glances at Marcus and Warren. "Mr. Ryann is new to the business. I assume you'll better inform him on how to behave before our next visit."

"We apologize," Warren replies, glancing at me sideways. "We'll leave him at home next time if you prefer."

"That won't be necessary," he answers. "Use this as a lesson learned," he tells me. "You won't get off so easily, if there's a next time." He's inches from my face. I swallow then give a small nod.

"We'll keep you posted, Mr. Valdez," Marcus interrupts— probably afraid I'm going to mess this up. He doesn't have to worry. I'm too busy thinking about how to help the girl without endangering Reese in the process.

"Tell Glenn I'll be waiting," he replies, heading toward a vehicle.

Marcus and Warren guide me to the car.

"Hands off. I'm fine," I tell them through gritted teeth.

Valdez yells over his shoulder. "Be careful, Mr. Ryann." A wry grin stretches his features. "Your physical strength won't get you very far here," he warns.

I watch him climb into the SUV, then one by one they drive away.

"**D**o you have any idea how much power he has in his pinky alone?" Marcus asks. "Nobody challenges Valdez the way you did."

We've been driving through the desert for about twenty minutes. We're on our way to see my father, who's been spending a lot of time with Rachelle—the woman I saw him with the other night. I assume she has him by the balls. I've never seen my father with the same woman twice, with the exception of my mother.

"Dude, I about shit my pants when he hit Salinas. I wasn't sure if any of us would live after that," Warren chuckles.

"Yeah, well, next time tell me what I'm up against."

"Rules are rules," Marcus replies.

I let out a sardonic laugh. "Is that why Valdez put a bullet in Salinas's head?"

"Valdez is crazy," he retorts. "You're lucky he didn't give you one to match."

A flash of something catches my eye, and I check out the back window, spotting a German shepherd wandering through the desert. It may be spring, but it's hot, and there's no way that dog will survive without water.

"Guys, turn around."

Marcus eyes me through the rearview, furrowing his brows. "You lose something?"

"No. I'm about to gain a dog."

# 6

## Reese

'm digging through my collection of DVDs, looking for the self-defense instructional 'After School Special,' I planned to show to the kids. I promised my dad I'd meet him for coffee before my shift, and I have to be at work in a couple hours. I'm running out of time. We skipped last week ... and I miss him. His persistence finally wore off, and I decided to give him a chance. We've gotten closer these last few months, though I still keep my guard up. It's hard to completely trust anyone.

"You're not cancelling on me, are you?" my dad answers on the first ring. There's a smile in his voice.

"No, I'm just running behind." Digging through the last of the DVDs, I finally find it. "Never mind." I look at the clock. "I'll be there in ten." I grin. "I'll explain when I get there. See you soon."

"All right. Don't break the speed limit for me. I can wait."

"I won't." I hang up the phone, with the DVD in tow, then make my way to my car.

Traffic is smooth, and I'm thankful. Ever since the conversation with Gia this morning, my anxiety has been through the roof. I'm nervous about the way things will play out tonight. Dinner's set for six. Gia told me Logan took the news exceptionally well, and that's what has me worried. He's not the type to give up without putting up a fight. So what is he doing? Is he really *that* concerned over temporarily losing his sexual privileges? My gut tells me *no*. I pull into a parking space close to the front and cut off the engine. The aroma of fresh coffee and pastries hit me like a tidal wave the moment I step inside. I let my eyes search the room enjoying the scent as I breathe it all in. It only takes a few seconds for me to find him, sitting at a table, alone in the corner. He has a full beard covering his face; it doesn't suit him. Our eyes meet, and he smiles, then I give him a little wave, making my way to the table. He hands me his credit card.

"Get me the usual. Black. No cream this time." He's never let me pay, so I've given up on trying. Plus, I think it makes him feel good to finally take the role he missed when I was a child.

I place our orders, and wait 'til they're ready before I take the seat across from him, sipping my latte with a grin. "Can I be honest?"

He nods. "Of course."

"I don't like the beard," I say, closing an eye, hoping I didn't offend him.

"You don't?" He runs a hand over it, squeezing with his finger and thumb. "What don't you like about it?" he asks, but he's smiling like he already knows.

"It ages you," I reply. "There's a handsome face under there. Why are you trying to hide it? You never were the facial hair type."

He shrugs. "I can always shave it off." He takes a sip of his coffee. "I just thought I'd try something different."

"Okay, fair enough." I nod, sipping on my latte. "You could at least trim it up a little." I can't help it. It looks awful. A couple of weeks ago when I had seen him, it was just a little more than stubble. Now it's a full-grown beard.

He laughs, and it reaches his belly. "Are you embarrassed to be seen with me?"

"No. Of course not." I feel bad. I'm happy to have him in my life again, and in no way am I embarrassed. "I'm just trying to help. You know … with the ladies."

His eyes crinkle at the sides. "Are you sure?"

"Stop it, Dad. You're making me feel bad."

He clears his throat. "Okay. No more teasing."

Oh my gosh. I just realized I called him dad. Now I feel awkward. It's the first time I've said it to his face.

"Reese." He places his hand over mine. "Thank you for giving me the chance at being your dad again. I hope one day you can forgive me, but I understand it takes time." He pats my hand with tears in his eyes. I blink mine away — not ready to talk about our past. I'd rather talk about now; it's easier. I smile. Thankfully, he changes the subject. "Have you heard from your mother?"

I sigh. "We talked last week — once since I saw you. She seems okay." I rest my chin in my hand. "It's hard to tell what's really going on with her." She rarely answers her phone and never calls anymore.

He nods. "Did she ask for money?"

"No. I called her." She only calls me when she needs something.

"Tell her to call me if she does. I'll take care of her."

"Shouldn't that be Tim's job?" I grumble. I bet he hasn't worked a day in his life.

Tilting his head, he says, "I'm not sure whose job it is," he replies. "It shouldn't be yours." He leans back in his chair and watches me. I nervously glance to the side. My stomach growls when I spot a blueberry muffin that calls my name—the kind with the frosting on top. My favorite. "I'm going to get something to eat," I tell him. I dart out of my chair not wanting him to pay for it, then quickly place the order. My mouth waters before I can sit back down. "I forgot to eat this morning," I tell him. I take a bite and moan—it's delicious.

"That why you were running late?" He raises his brows.

"Hmm? Oh … no." I place a hand over my mouth and swallow. "I was looking for a DVD on self-defense. I need it for class today." I take a sip of my coffee. "Do you want a bite?" I ask, offering him a piece of my muffin before I scarf it all down.

He shakes his head. "No, thank you."

"Thank God." I smile. "'Cause this is *way* too good to share." Both of us laugh.

His expression changes to serious, and he clears his throat. The concern on his face begins to worry me.

"What is it?"

"I've been meaning to ask," he says, folding his hands. "Did you ever hear from that boy you were dating, the old neighbor?"

I shake my head. "Everything's still the same." I frown. "He hasn't contacted me." Just like that, my mood turns sour.

"You haven't heard from him at all?"

"Nope." I drop my gaze to the table, unable to look him in the eye. I'm embarrassed.

He sips on his coffee. "So what's next then?"

"What do you mean?" I furrow my brows.

"Will you wait for him?"

"He basically sent me a Dear John letter. There's nothing to wait for." I play with my cup.

He watches me carefully, making me nervous. "Is there

someone else?" It's like I'm being interrogated.

"Are you going to arrest me if I answer that?"

He laughs. "It's the investigator in me. I don't mean to be nosey. I'm still learning how to be a dad." He winks, making me grin.

I give him what he wants. "Well, there's this friend." I pause, chew on my lip. "He's been good to me the last few months. I'm having him over for dinner tonight, which is a step." I lift my brows. "It's sort of like a double date thing."

He smiles, but it doesn't reach his eyes. "It could be a nice distraction."

"A distraction," I say, tilting my head. "What do you mean?" I glance at the time. "Shoot! I need to go."

He scoots out his chair. "Let me walk you."

"So, what are your big plans for the night?"

His eyes crinkle at the sides. "I'm going to church." He shrugs, hands in his pockets. The man I knew before would have never stepped foot in church. The changes I see in him continue to blow my mind. "Why the face?"

"I just never thought I'd see the day—*you* going to church," I tell him.

He nods. "I guess I learned that life's too big to handle without a little help." He leans in and gives me a warm hug.

"Thanks for the coffee," I tell him.

"Have a good day at work. You be careful."

"I will."

His voice shakes nervously when he says, "I love you."

I'm still not comfortable telling him those words. "Okay, bye." I climb in and start the engine, watching his reflection disappear as I make my way out of the parking lot.

"That seat's taken," Logan says from his chair. Gia and I prepared a spaghetti and meatball dinner, with salad and French bread.

Sean freezes in his spot. He's holding a full plate of food, trying to decide if Logan means it. Knowing Logan, he means every word. He wants to be an ass, and he's good at it.

I shoot daggers from across the table, grabbing Sean by the arm, tugging lightly. "You can sit. Logan's kidding."

"No, I'm not. That's Luke's spot," Logan replies, pointing his fork in Sean's direction. The table moves abruptly when Gia kicks him, but he doesn't even flinch, like it's something he prepared for. She and I exchange a worried glance.

"Speaking of Luke," Sean replies, buttering his bread. "Where is he? It's funny, I can't seem to get a straight answer out of Reese." His eyes move from Logan to me. "Does he disappear often?" There's no hiding the bite in his tone. I want to crawl under the table and hide. This is *not* what I had in mind.

As I try to think of a way to change the subject, Logan says, "Why don't you ask him, when he gets back and finds you moving in on his girl?"

Gia fakes a laugh. "You're such a jokester. Would anybody like a glass of wine?" The last part nearly comes out as a growl. She glares at Logan, but he doesn't spare her a glance. There's a challenge in both boys' expressions. The testosterone is thickening by the second.

I glance at Sean who's back to enjoying his food like nothing ever happened. "Do you like it?" I ask.

He grins. "The sauce is amazing." Getting another fork full

and shoving it into his mouth, he wiggles his brows. "Really good." He gives Gia a thumbs-up.

"It's my secret recipe," she replies, coming from a long line of talented chefs in her family.

"She's a natural." I smile. Wish I could say the same for myself.

Sean leans over and whispers, "Was your job to put the bread in the oven?" I elbow him in the arm. I've never been much of a cook, which I've told him before. His eyes sparkle, and he tells Gia, "I'd love it if you let me in on your secret."

"Not gonna happen," Logan snorts. "Ow!" His head snaps over to Gia. She glares at him. If looks could kill …

"Have I mentioned that you ladies look lovely tonight?" Sean's gaze moves from Gia to me, then he winks, obviously trying to change the subject.

"Thank you," we both reply at the same time.

"Douche." Logan fakes a cough loud enough so that all of us can hear. I'm mortified. Gia's mouth has reached the floor. Logan is staring at Sean, who is smirking at his plate, as though he finds this funny.

"Logan, can I see you privately for a moment?" I ask, completely livid. My eyes flick to Gia, and she nods. She'll be punishing him later. I have no doubt about that.

"Love to," he answers.

"Excuse me, Sean." I scoot out my chair. He takes a full bite of spaghetti, behaving as if what just happened is normal. I storm down the hall and pinch the bridge of my nose. Logan is behind me when I turn around. "What are you're doing?" I whisper yell.

He grins. "What does it look like I'm doing?"

Placing my hands on my hips, I tell him, "You're being completely immature. I swear, what you just did in there was like something straight out of elementary school!"

"I don't like him." He shrugs.

Gia prances down the hall, holding a glass of wine in her hand. She's pissed and on a mission, immediately getting in Logan's face. "No sex for you! Forget it." Then she walks into her room and slams the door.

My eyes flick to Logan's. "Great! He came here to eat alone. Thanks for making him feel welcome. I appreciate it." I stride down the hall toward the kitchen, but Logan stops me with his words.

"What exactly do you think Luke is doing?"

"No idea." *Why don't you tell me?* I want to say. I think all of us know that he isn't where he said he'd be.

"You think he's with another chick?" I don't respond, but the possibility has definitely run through my mind. "You really don't have a clue, do you?" He scoffs, letting out a sardonic laugh. "You're it for him. He's in love with you."

Momentarily squeezing my eyes shut, I reopen then and leave him alone in the hall. Sean sits at the table with half a glass of wine and an empty plate in front of him. I clear our dishes then place them in the sink—a little shaky and embarrassed. "I'm sorry dinner was," I purse my lips, trying to find the appropriate words, " cut a little short."

He smiles. "Dinner was amazing. Don't worry about it."

I sigh. "I wasn't expecting him to be rude like that. It was completely uncalled for."

Rubbing his belly, he yawns. "It's not your fault. And hey, I got a meal out of it. Beats Ramen any night." He raises his brows. "I should probably get going though, considering those two are about to fight," he says, pointing toward the hall.

I look in that direction and blow out a breath. "Yeah. I guess you're right. In fact, I think I can hear them now."

"You're welcome to join me if you want?"

"It's tempting, but I'm tired. Next time we'll have to—"

"Go out," he interrupts. "You're gonna let me take you out, right? Saturday?" He winks.

"Yes. And I'm looking forward to it." I nod. "Plus, I made you a promise, remember?"

He walks toward the door, stretching. "And I'm going to hold you to that promise."

"You do that," I tell him. We say our goodbyes, and I finish cleaning the remnants of our dinner, while listening to the faint sounds of Logan and Gia's fight. This is going to be a long night.

# 1

## Luke

Time. That's what my father wants from me. It's not about the money—never has been. No. For him, it's all about payback. It's about getting even for the time he's lost. After all, I was the one who turned us in that day—the day I saw my mother's charred remains pulled out from the rubble.

I'd walked out the front door, sick of listening to them argue. She'd begged and pleaded that I not go, though the pleading was with my father. I didn't have a choice in the matter. It was the last time I'd see her alive.

They'd hauled us off in separate vehicles—him to prison, me to juvie. I'd thought leading them to the drugs would lighten the guilt I'd felt for leaving her. The judge let me off easy. My father didn't get the same leniency. They'd tacked on a bunch of extra charges for child abuse and neglect, which only lengthened his sentence.

The fire was ruled an accident, and they never reopened the case. Lauren and I were placed into the foster system where we continued to have our ups and downs, but for the most part things were better.

I glance at my furry companion who's taking up residency in

my bed. "Glad you're comfy." He snores beside me. He's been here all of forty-eight hours and clearly made himself at home. We took a liking to each other right off the bat. Maybe he sensed he could trust me—that he needed me as much as I needed him. They say dogs are good at those things. The chances of finding him were slim to none, but we did. I glance at his sable-colored coat and scratch him on the neck. "Chance."

His ears twitch, and he watches me, with eyes that are almost human. Maybe that's why I talk to him like he is. Either that or I'm crazy.

"You like that name?"

He raises his head then tilts it.

I'll take that as a *yes*. "Chance it is," I murmur, turning over. "Do me a favor and scoot over. You're hogging the bed."

My cell phone chirps with a text while he pants beside me. I glance at the clock. "Looks like you're alone tonight, buddy." A minute later it's ringing. There are only a handful of people who would call—none who I want to talk to, but I place the phone against my ear anyway. "What do you want?" I grumble.

"We found Samuel," Warren replies from the other end.

I rake my hand through my hair, staring at the bare wall across from me. I've only had an hour of sleep.

"Meet us at the shop. Hurry."

I know this won't end well for him, regardless if he took the money or not. "Be there in twenty," I mumble back. Warren hesitates like there's something more to say, but the line clicks, and he's gone. I drop the phone on the bed and look at Chance who's watching me with disapproval.

"What?" I ask. He gets up on all fours then jumps off the bed and makes his way to the back door. I walk over and let him out, fill up his food, then put in a call to Andrew.

The Smoke Shop is a business my father uses as a cover right outside of Tucson. Marcus and Warren stand outside looking like they haven't slept any more than I have.

Warren flicks his cigarette to the ground before immediately lighting another. "Gage has got him in the back," he says, his head tipping toward the entrance. The door swings open, and my father walks out with Rachelle close behind him. She's dressed like a two-dollar hooker.

"Glad you could finally make it," he grumbles, disappointed I'm the last one here.

"Anything for you, *Dad*," I bite back.

"Luuuke," Rachelle sighs, wrapping her arms around me. "It's so good to see you." She presses her entire body against me. My father seems to enjoy the interaction, which only confuses me. I break away without a word, clearing my throat. The guys snicker beside me.

"We were just leaving," my father says, unlocking his car. "Gage knows what to do."

"Of course he does," I tell him, rocking back on my heels.

"Goodbye, son." They both climb inside his Range Rover, and we watch them drive away.

"She wants you," Warren says, blowing out a cloud of smoke. "And your dad don't seem to mind either."

My mouth tips at the corners. "Not my type," I murmur back. Marcus and Warren both chuckle, as I push past them and step inside the shop. I follow a trail of blood that leads me directly to a tied up Samuel. Gage holds a knife in his hand and hovers over him. He's got that strung out look in his eyes. My gaze falls to the ground where I spot a couple of sawed off fingers and a lot of blood.

"Tell me," Gage growls, then grabs him by the collar. "Where is the money?" Samuel tries to speak, but he's gagged. I can't make out a word he's saying. Gage takes the knife to another finger.

Samuel's face pales, and his eyes widen as he screams. He's already lost a couple pints of blood.

"You're going to kill him before he has a chance," I spit. "Take out the gag."

"You think you can do better?" Gage places a cigarette between his lips and gets in my face. "Be my guest," he says, bumping my shoulder as he walks out of the room. "Five minutes," he grumbles. I watch him 'til he's gone, then turn to Samuel and bend down so we're eye to eye.

"Look, I need you to be honest with me, Samuel." I gesture over my shoulder. "You want him to rape your wife … kill your children?" I ask, untying the gag.

"Please, you've got to believe me," he says.

I watch as beads of sweat cover his face. "We paid them a visit the other day. If you care about your family, you'll tell us everything. Where is the money?"

One of his eyes is swollen shut, and his face is bloody. "I told him," he moans. "I had the money — went where they told me to go, waited about fifteen minutes. Nobody came," he replies convincingly. "I called Glenn and asked him if there was some kind of miscommunication." He swallows. "Then, before I knew it, everything went black." He shakes his head. "You've got to believe me," he pleads. "Please, don't let them hurt my family. They're innocent!"

"If someone took the money, why'd they leave you alive? What would be the point?" I ask.

"I don't know … to buy time maybe. To make me look guilty. C'mon, it makes sense!" His eyes widen. "You could be out looking for them, but instead you're wasting time on me!"

"Who took it?" Gage asks from behind me. Marcus and Warren stand beside him.

Samuel looks out of steam. "I told you, the cartel. Untie me, man. It wasn't me. Valdez took the money!"

"He's worked with Glenn for years. Why would *he* do it?" Gage replies.

"Because he's evil!" Samuel cries. "Everyone knows that."

"Not good enough." A second later there's a loud pop. I crouch down to the floor and hear several more.

"What the hell, man?" I glance over my shoulder. Gage stands, pointing his gun towards Samuel's now executed body, ready to unleash some more. I look down and find his blood all over me. The rest of it drains from his body to the floor.

"I think you got him," Marcus grumbles before Gage releases a couple more.

I walk out of the room, my blood boiling, my head ready to explode.

"Where are you going?" Gage asks.

Pressing my lips into a tight line, I turn to face him. "That wasn't your call in there." I point back to the room. My fists are clenched tight. I can barely stand to look at him. If Andrew doesn't come through with some news, I'm going to crack.

A menacing grin crosses his face. "You sayin' it was yours?" he asks, lifting his brows.

"I'm saying I believed him. I'm saying he didn't have to die." Filthy prick.

"He lost the money. If Glenn doesn't get paid, we don't get paid. I'm not sure about you, but when it comes to food on the table, there ain't any room for second chances."

"You and I are nothing alike," I reply, pushing out the exit.

He follows behind. "C'mon. We got shit to do." He walks down the road and breaks into a silver Honda, placing the AK in the back.

I cock a brow. "What kind of shit?"

His head tips toward the shop. "They'll take care of the body."

That wasn't an answer, and I need to get as far away from him as possible. I do a once over of my appearance, still covered in Samuel's blood. "Nah, I'm going home. I need a shower."

The corner of his mouth tips. "You'll have to wait. We aren't finished."

"Finish without me. You can handle it." My eyes move to the weapon in the back.

"Handle it I can, but your father has orders. It's time to prove your loyalty. You think you're ready to do that?"

My eyes narrow. "Are you shitting me? Haven't I done that already?" I make my way around the car, then get in and slam the door, knowing there's no way around this.

Gage cackles before driving us away. "You sure you want me to answer that?" His eyes stay on the road. We merge to the right and take the highway that leads to Phoenix.

"Where the hell are we going?" My heart rate quickens. I don't want this guy anywhere near Reese—not even in the same city. The same state is too close.

"Tying up some loose ends." He purses his lips. "You don't have any loose ends, do ya, Luke?"

"What are you talking about? No, I don't have any loose ends," I reply.

He laughs. "Oh, I think you do." His hands tighten on the wheel.

"Phoenix is a *two*-hour drive. What's so important that it can't wait until tomorrow?" I'm not playing his game.

"Samuel's wife knows too much. Glenn wants us to take care of her."

"Kill her, you mean?"

"Something, like that," he says, and grabbing his dick, adds, "Though I plan on having a little fun with her first."

I stare out the windshield shaking my head, thinking about Samuel's pleas. "Their kids will become orphans."

He laughs. "That's where you come in. You can do it in their sleep." He nods. "They'll never know what happened."

I scrub my face with my hands. Are you kidding me? "Glenn wanted this?" Of course he did.

Handing me his phone, he says, "You want to ask him?" I'm not sure why this surprises me.

I toss it back. "I don't need to call him." Shutting my eyes, I think of a way to contact Andrew. We need to get his family out of there. But our only source of communication is back in the attic, which is a shame since nobody bothered to check me tonight. It's the first time they haven't searched me from head to toe since I started. *Damn, I need that phone.*

I look out the window and spot a gas station. An idea comes to my mind. "Pull over at the Chevron, so I can piss."

"We're not far enough out. I don't want to chance it."

I growl. "Chance what? You want me to piss all over the car? Pull over." I need to find a payphone, somewhere out of view. If he gets suspicious, he'll go straight to Glenn. For whatever reason, he's his little puppet, yet he's made it clear he hates him. Maybe it's a, 'keep your enemies closer' kind of thing. Either way, this could all blow up in my face. He'd know I was up to something, which I have no doubt could put Reese in danger. He'd kill her to make a point—maybe more. It's been instilled in my brain all of my life. *Nobody fucks with Glenn Ryann.* But I'm changing the rules. He threatened the woman I love, and it's a line he's going to wish he never crossed. I'll make sure of it.

"You're gonna have to wait another twenty minutes. You can piss on the side of the road." We pass the exit for the gas station. I want to slam my fist in his face again, but I force myself to stay calm.

At least an hour rolls by before Gage pulls over between Phoenix and Casa Grande. Too wrapped up in my thoughts, I hadn't noticed how much time had passed. Plus, I'd lied about needing to piss in the first place. Now it feels like a good idea. I get out of the car and shut the door. Gage follows behind. Neither of us walks far to relieve ourselves, then we climb back into the car—minutes away from our destination.

My nerves are shot. It's hard not knowing how the next hour will play out. What Gage is planning to do? And how far they want me to go to prove myself. Do they expect me to turn into some twisted fuck like the rest of them? I can't do that.

We pull into the complex, and Gage kills the engine. Both of us step outside, neither one of us speaking. It couldn't be any more desolate right now. Talk about the perfect set up. The asshole doesn't waste any time, striding down the path leading directly to their apartment. He pulls out a set of keys, unlocking the door on the third try. He must have taken them from Samuel.

We walk around the apartment in the dark, not bothering to flip on the lights. Gage has his back to me when I knock a couple pictures off the wall, and they make a loud crash. I hold up my hands like it was an accident. Gage shoves me back. I'm ready to fight him right there, but he pulls out a gun from his waistband then shakes his head in warning.

I hear a creaking in the floor and wonder if it's the kids, their mother, or maybe both. Gage peeks around the corner. "I've got some business to take care of," he says, tipping his head. "Keep an eye on the kids. When I'm done you can have a turn." He thrusts his hips back and forth with a crooked smile.

"You're a sick son of a bitch. You know that?" My jaw clenches. I look over my shoulder at the room behind me, assuming it's where the kids are. Gage is more interested in the room to the right.

His grin grows wide. "After tonight, you'll be just as sick as I am." He turns and makes his way toward the bedroom.

I head into the other room and look for the kids, but their beds are empty. One side is decorated for a boy the other for a girl— Spiderman and Princesses or Fairies, whatever you call them. Whispers come from the closet. I close my eyes with a sinking feeling in my stomach, quietly shutting the door. For a moment I thought they'd escaped this, but no such luck.

I open the closet and press a finger to my lips, seeing the fear in their wide eyes. The girl clutches a blanket like it's her lifeline. Her brother tries to comfort her. I have a flashback of my sister and I around the same age.

"I'm not going to hurt you," I whisper to the girl. I don't think she believes me. Her chocolate-colored hair hangs in ringlets. "Can I borrow your brother for a second?" She just watches me and doesn't answer. I wasn't really expecting her to. I walk over to the window and slide it open. Noises come from the other room, each of them turning toward their door. They know something's happening to their mother.

"I'm going to keep you safe. I promise," I say, showing them my palms. "But you're going to have to listen to me, all right?" The girl nods, which is progress. The boy steps out of the closet. I pull him to the side. "You like Spiderman, right?" He nods again, then his sister starts to cry when she hears her mother's muffled screams. My adrenaline picks up.

"Listen." I grab his shoulders. "I need you to be Spiderman tonight. It's very important that you save your sister. Can you do that for me?"

He glances at the door. "Is someone hurting my mom?"

"That's what I'm going to find out." My eyes flick to the girl. "You worry about your sister, and I'll take care of your mom."

I wave the girl over with a shaky hand. "Come out of the closet, sweetie." She hesitates, afraid. There's no reason for her to trust me, but they need to get out of here now.

"Come on, Izzy," her brother says. "He's not a bad guy." She slowly creeps out of the closet, and I rush them to the window. One after the other I help them out, leaving the rest of the responsibility to the brother. Either way, they'll be safer.

I lean out the window. "Do you have a friend who lives nearby?"

"Yeah," the boy answers, taking his sister's hand.

"Take Izzy and go there," I whisper. "Don't come back. Wait for your mother or me. We'll find you." He nods, and they run away hand in hand.

I close the window and make my way down the hall. The door is partly cracked. Pushing it open, I step inside. Gage, with his back to me, is holding the gun against the woman's head. She's naked and kneeling in front of him, tears spilling down her cheeks. My jaw tightens. I'd love to take that gun, shove it up his ass, and pull the trigger.

"Stop crying, bitch, and do as you're told," he growls, grabbing a fist full of her hair. "Or I'll wake up your kids and make them watch?"

Her eyes widen. "No! Please don't. Don't hurt my babies. I'll do anything," she cries. "Anything you want!"

"That's better," he says, tugging on her hair again. He slowly slides the gun away from her temple and frees himself from his jeans.

I sneak up behind him and reach for the gun, but he spots me right before I'm able to grab it. Instead, I knock it out of his hand. He dives for it, and I tackle him, slamming him into the dresser.

"You're dead, Ryann," he hisses. We both fall to the ground. I hammer him with each of my fists, and we bump into some furniture. Something heavy lands on my face and shatters. I shake it off, trying to grab the gun, but Gage is there before me. He has it cocked and ready to shoot. "Say goodbye, Romeo."

"Eat shit, you pathetic waste of a human." I shove his hand away, climbing on top of him, prying his fingers off the gun. All I see is red—the woman on her knees with her tearstained face, the little girl in the closet, a younger version of Reese with her hands tied behind her back, her cries for help. I pound a fist into his face over and over again. Then the gun goes off, and I still—not knowing if I'm shot.

Gage's body goes limp beneath me. The gun is now in my hand, free from his grip. I slide off him and back away so I'm leaning against the foot of the bed. He's bleeding out all over the carpet. My eyes lift to his face, and it only confirms what I feared. Gage is dead, and I'm the one who killed him.

"Take a little," I tell her. "Trust me, I have plenty more." The cash is in my hand, but she refuses to take it. After helping her find her kids, she was kind enough to lend me her phone, her shower, and a clean pair of clothes.

She continues to thank me. "You've done enough. We don't need it."

The feds will be here any minute, and the family will be taken into protective custody, where they belong. We hear a ringing in the other room, reminding me of what I did.

I glance at her. "Is that yours?"

She shakes her head, then her eyes widen.

I turn around and make my way into the room. My gaze falls on Gage's dead body. "Shit!" The ringing is coming from his pants. I'm not sure what to do. I lean over and pat down his pockets. When I find it, Marcus's number flashes across the screen. I rake a hand through my hair and panic.

If I don't answer, they'll sense something is wrong and probably come down here. If they figure it out, they'll go after Reese just to spite me. That leaves me with no choice. I flip open the phone.

"Took you long enough," Marcus groans. He sounds tired. "You guys finished?"

"Not yet." My words are clipped.

"Well, what's taking you so long? Never mind, don't answer that. Anyway, my work is done. I'm going to bed. I'll talk to your perverted ass tomorrow."

My tension fades a little. "Later." I flip the phone shut and pinch the bridge of my nose. That could have gone a lot worse.

A minute later I'm giving my condolences and saying my goodbyes.

# 8

## Reese

I spent at least thirty minutes in the shower, hoping, by the time I got out, Logan and Gia would be over their little spat. Thankfully, things have died down. Slipping into one of Luke's old t-shirts, I replay Logan's earlier words in my head. Our conversation in the hall is really starting to get to me—that and his confidence that Luke still loves me. Why does part of me feel guilty for thinking any less?

I cover my legs in lotion then turn off the light, moving toward my bed, nearly tripping over what feels to be a large pair of shoes—a pair of shoes I realize are not mine. Half of me stills when I spot someone sitting on my bed, but the other half recognizes him immediately—from the squared jawline to his thick, muscular build. There's a familiarity permeating the air that only his presence brings. Electricity crackles between us, and goose bumps prick the back of my neck. I cover my mouth with shaky hands. "What …what are you doing here?" My heart triples its normal pace.

His head is in his hands, and he hasn't moved or made an effort to look at me. How *dare* he show up like this without warning. I'm so angry I could physically attack him. Why isn't he saying anything? Do I remind him that this is over … make him get out? Do I give him a chance to explain? Our only light comes from the moon shining through the window, though I'd recognize his shadow from anywhere. A single tear makes its way down my cheek. I resist the urge to wipe it away. He doesn't deserve to know the power he still has over me.

"Answer me, damn it!" I yell. "If you're not going to speak, you should leave!"

When those brown eyes lift to mine, there's a sinking in my stomach. I run over and flip on the light; scared, I slowly walk toward him. His appearance makes me gasp. His eyes are red and swollen, as if he's been crying. There are strange little cuts on his face—not the kind that come from fighting. They don't look like he got them in the cage.

His expression holds so much anguish that it terrifies the living hell out of me. I can see that he's in pain, and not just the physical kind. It's much worse. The sight of him breaks my heart, and my walls quickly crumble.

I reach out and cup his face, trembling on the way. "My God, Luke, what happened to you?" I gasp, feeling my anger dissipate.

He's gazing at me as if it's the last time he'll ever see me, then he shuts his eyes and wraps his arms around me, pulling me down on the bed. The action surprises me. "I'm so sorry," he says, full of emotion. "I'm *so* sorry. You've got to believe me." He rests his head in my lap, his face pressed against my stomach, and starts to weep. I'm frozen by the rawness and vulnerability of it all.

His tears seep through my shirt, onto my skin. I'm biting back my own, softly stroking his hair with my fingers. His arms clench me tighter, and I lean down to kiss the top of his head. It's amazing how much I want to slap and kiss this man at the same time.

I have no idea where he's been or what has happened, and it's taking every part of me not to ask. I need to be patient. I know this. I can see it in his eyes. Whatever he's apologizing for has got to do with much more than our past. He made the decision to leave; no one forced him into anything. I want to know what's going on—hoping he'll tell me when he's ready.

After a few more minutes of his crying, the room is silent. I try to think of something I can say before he beats me to it, breathing me in.

"You smell like home." He tightens his arms around me. "I'm probably the last person you want to talk to, but I couldn't stay away." There's desperation in his voice. "I had to see you."

Looking down on his pain-stricken face, I want to tell him that I've missed him, but I can't bring myself to say it. "Luke, you're scaring me." I've never seen him like this before.

He closes his eyes. "My head isn't in a good place," he says, turning onto his back. "Then seeing you sort of turned me into a pussy." He swallows. "I've missed you."

I'm trying not to cry. It feels so good to hear that he's missed me, too. "How long are you here?"

He tucks my hair behind my ear. "I leave tomorrow."

"I haven't heard from you in months, and when I do, you show up like this?" Shaking my head, I continue. "I want to help, but you have to let me, Luke." My lip involuntarily quivers. I can no longer hold it back.

He brushes the pad of his thumb over my cheeks, wiping away my tears. "I hate that I do this to you." There's concern in his gaze. "There's so much I want to tell you," he says, raising his brows. "And I *will* tell you when this is over." He sits up and places his hands on my shoulders, forcing me to meet his eyes.

"It's not about letting you in, Reese." He pauses. "You're already here." Taking my hand, he holds it over his heart. "That's never going to change."

I furrow my brows and scoot away from him. "Then why would you send me that letter? This isn't a game, Luke. This is my heart." I rest back against the headboard, crossing my arms defensively.

He takes the spot beside me, stretching out his legs. "You're right. This isn't a game." He turns toward me. "It never was." He blows out a breath, looking stressed as he frowns. "I realized I wasn't being fair to you—expecting you to wait. I couldn't even give you an explanation." I give him a sideways glance, and he raises his brows. "I was giving you an out," he tells me, tucking my hair behind my ear. "I was trying to do the right thing," he sighs, resigning.

I break away from his gaze, pondering this new information. "And what about now?"

"Now?"

I nod. "You still trying to do the right thing? Give me an out?"

He rests his head against the headboard. His eyes move to the ceiling. "You want honesty?"

"Always," I reply softly.

He clenches his jaw. "The thought of another man touching you," he says, shaking his head. "I can't even describe the rage it brings. Deep down, I was hoping the letter wouldn't matter," he swallows. "But the truth is, in the end," he turns to face me, his gaze intense, "if I have to fight for you, I will, no matter which path you choose, because the way I see it, you're mine. You'll always be mine."

His eyes fall to my lips. I'm wondering if he's going to kiss me. They continue to travel down my neck, locking on my chest, and the corner of his mouth tips slightly. He's noticed I'm wearing his shirt. My stomach is doing flip-flops, and my entire body tingles from his words. I can't help it. I'm completely turned on. "Boy, you sure are full of yourself, aren't you?" I want him to kiss me. I want him to touch me in places he's never touched before. No, I don't. Yes, I do. No, I don't. *Ugh.* I just want him.

"How so?"

"You're telling me I don't get a say in this." I can't pretend like Luke didn't leave me here on a lie, just because he has a weak moment, and my hormones are raging. He still needs to produce some answers.

"You'll always get a say." He watches me carefully.

I place a pillow on top of my lap and fold my hands. "What if you don't like what I have to say?" I lift my chin and look him in the eye, pretending to be strong, but I'm weakening by the second.

He takes a lock of my hair, watching it as he twists it around his finger. "Then I'll do whatever it takes to change your mind." He licks his lips. "I'm not afraid to face the challenge, if that's what you're asking." He looks into my eyes. "When I want something I fight for it." He tucks the hair behind my ear. "And what I want is *you.*"

My breathing quickens. Everything about him screams sincerity, but my mind warns me to be careful. "If I ask you something, will you give me a straight answer?" I ask nervously.

His body goes rigid. "It depends on what you ask." By the look on his face, he's just as irritated with his reply as I am.

It's hard to meet his gaze. "You never went to Brazil, did you?" I'm embarrassed I fell for the lie.

I hear him release a breath before he says, "Look at me," pulling my face toward his with his finger and thumb. I slowly lock eyes with him. The heat in his gaze makes my pulse race unnaturally. I feel the electricity crackling between us.

"I shouldn't have lied to you." He presses his lips into a tight line. "The letter about Brazil just happened to be there at the right time, and I took it as an easy out."

"But why?" I want so badly to understand.

Running a hand over his face, he continues. "Because if I'd told you the truth, you would have gotten in the middle of it."

"How do you know?"

"Because you're stubborn!" His eyes widen, and he shakes his head. "You know it. I know it. It's one of the things I love about you. But it drives me crazy at the same time." The corner of his mouth tips, making me frown. "Listen." He lifts my chin. "I swear to you. I'm going to tell you everything." His eyes are intent on making me believe him, and I want to. I want to with all that is in me.

I nervously chew on my lip. "Is what you're doing dangerous? Is that why you're being so secretive? Why you don't want me involved?" I think about the Taser he sent me. It's the only explanation I can come up with.

"For you." There's tension in his jaw. "That's all I can tell you right now. I'm sorry. You're just going to have to accept that."

I close my eyes, hoping it isn't something illegal, or something that could get him killed, then shake away the thought—for my own sanity. I have to trust him. I know he's a good man. "Just don't lie to me again," I murmur. "You have no idea how much this has hurt me—how gullible it makes me feel." *How ridiculously stupid and naïve. Should I go on?*

"I promise." His gaze softens, and he cups my face. "It was never my intention to hurt you." Looking into my eyes, he continues, "You know that, right?"

Hesitating, I finally say, "You've got to understand. This is going to be hard for me, and I still have questions."

"You should." He nods. "But right now, I'm going to need you to trust me." There's compassion in his eyes. I gaze at the various cuts all over his handsome face.

"Will you tell me what happened to your face?"

A flicker of pain settles over his features. He pauses. "If I answer, will you answer a question for me?"

"That sounds fair." I cross my arms and get comfortable.

His eyes are on the bed as he runs his hand across the stubble on his chin. "A lamp."

My brows bunch together. "A lamp?" Definitely not the answer I was expecting.

His gaze moves to mine. "Yeah … a lamp." He leans over and smells me closing his eyes. "I got into brawl tonight." He leans back. "We bumped into some furniture. The lamp fell over, and I caught it in the face." His eyes are far away.

I examine the cuts and bruises. "You *caught* it in the face?"

"Yeah." He nods. "Something like that." There's so much he's not telling me.

"Did you kick his ass?" I scoot down and lay my head on the pillow. He does the same beside me. Now we're lying on our sides facing each other.

Clenching his jaw, he replies, "I took care of it." His eyes flick over my shoulder then he adds, "My turn to ask questions."

"What do you want to know?" I arch a brow. I don't really have any secrets.

He runs the back of his knuckles over the side of my face. "Has Logan been taking care of you?"

I give him my best glare. "By the way, thank you for that," I grumble.

His mouth turns into a half grin. "What?"

Swatting him on the arm, I tell him, "The man drives me crazy." He raises his brows waiting for more. "First of all, he's extremely nosey."

He fakes innocence, but I'm not stupid. He's the one who told Logan to watch out for me in the first place. "What's he nosey about?"

I'm not sure how to answer that. He's mainly nosey about Sean, and I don't feel comfortable talking about Sean with the man lying next to me. In fact, Luke doesn't like Sean even a little bit. And to make matters worse, he happens to be his landlord. "About everything," I finally reply. "He's just nosey ... and he tries to get me to spar with him at the gym."

His mouth tips up at the corners. "And you won't?"

"Of course not," I scoff. "I understand you're concerned, but I don't need a sitter, and I'm *definitely* not wrestling with Logan," I murmur.

He releases a throaty laugh. It may be at my expense, but I'm happy to finally hear it. "So work must be a real breeze for you then?" He teases with a twinkle in his eye.

"Ugh, it's awful. And now that Logan practically lives here, I have to listen to his sex-capades with my best friend in the next room. I can never catch a break!"

"Oh, come on," he says, tipping his head back. "It can't be that bad." He's softly running his palm over my thigh. I want him to keep it there.

I grin. "But it is." My eyes fall on his handsome dimples.

He reaches over to brush the hair off my face. "Now there's the smile I love to see." He tenderly touches my cheek. I try to pretend these simple touches don't affect me, but they do.

"I wish I could understand why you're doing this," I murmur.

"Why you have to leave? All of this."

His gaze falls to my mouth, and he leans in. "Do you trust me?"

I lick my lips unconsciously. I wonder if he feels the same pull that I do whenever we're near each other. "I want to."

He looks hurt. "Why is that so hard for you to do?" He furrows his brows. "Have I ever intentionally hurt you? Think about it. You know me, Reese. When have I not had your best interest at heart?"

I'm afraid I don't know how to answer that, so I reach out and squeeze his hand. "No more lies, Luke."

He squeezes mine back with understanding in his eyes. "No more lies," he replies.

# 9

## Reese

I blink my eyes awake and find Luke lying across from me, watching me. I don't even remember falling asleep. We were talking about my life since his absence. I filled him in on work, Logan taking over the class, and how the kids were still constantly asking about him. Somehow the conversation moved to my dad. After that, things get a little blurry. My eyes fill with tears from the bittersweet realization that he's here, but he's leaving in the morning. I don't know when I'll get to see him again.

"You look peaceful when you sleep," he tells me.

"How long have I been out?"

He glances at the clock. "Thirty minutes, if that."

I sit up and fold my legs behind me. "Sorry. I didn't realize I was nodding off."

He gives a half grin, but there's sadness in his eyes. "I like watching you sleep."

"I don't want to sleep. You're leaving."

He leans in and strokes my cheek tenderly. "I'm sorry." He swallows, then we stare at each other for a while, neither of us needing to speak to communicate what we're feeling.

"How 'bout you let me take care of your face?" I climb out

of bed and make my way into the bathroom. I peek over my shoulder, and his mouth curves into a partial grin.

"You going to nurse me back to health?"

"I'm going to try," I reply, crouching under the sink, searching for the first aid kit. I find it then place it onto the counter. "We're in luck," I say, relieved.

His tattooed arm flexes back to grip his shirt, then he pulls it over his head and steps toward me. It all sort of happens in slow motion. My eyes take their fill of his chest, before traveling down the tight ripples of his stomach, lingering on the sexy V that disappears into his jeans—I'm captivated.

I blink away my lust, clearing my throat. "I was going to say, you should probably take your shirt off for this." I can hear the nervousness in my voice. It's obvious I'm a twenty-one year old virgin. The man is only shirtless, and I'm already blushing.

Standing less than a foot away, he effortlessly lifts me onto the counter. I can instantly feel the chemistry between us the moment his fingertips meet my hips. Those eyes are going to trap me. I can tell he feels it, too. "You okay?" he asks softly, not realizing how much he's affecting me. He smells divine—like soap, mint, and everything Luke.

"Uh huh," I answer back, flustered, pouring the antiseptic onto some cotton, praying he doesn't read me. If he can be strong, so can I.

"You sure?"

"Yeah," I reply, doing what I can to keep my composure. My nerves are shot, and my heart is beating really fast. I'm desperate for him to kiss me, and wonder if he wants to kiss me, too. I gently dab the left side of his face. "Sorry, this may sting a little."

He places his hands on my thighs. "You're shaking." His warm breath blows over me.

"Really?" I pause. "Funny, I must be cold. Tell me if I'm hurting you. Okay?" Leaning forward, I blow on his cheek.

His thumbs rub circles over my thighs. The movement feels sensual. "You want me to get you a blanket?" I shake my head no, blowing on another area. I don't trust myself to speak. "That feels good," he says, moving his hands up and down my thighs, attempting to warm me up. "Your skin is really soft," he mumbles.

*Does he have any idea what he's doing to me?* Our closeness makes me tingly — add our lack of clothing, his hands on my thighs, and the thickness I hear in his voice, and I'm a mess. "Um, thanks. Can you turn your head a little," I murmur, finally looking into his eyes. That's when my mouth runs dry, and I suck in a breath. "Are you okay?"

His face is serious as he watches me with hungry eyes and closes the distance between us. He slightly shakes his head. "No," is all he says. He drops his face to the crook of my neck, rolling his forehead from side to side. I stretch my neck to give him better access, closing my eyes. His hands remain on my thighs, and he grips them tightly as if he's fighting for some control.

He inhales a long slow breath. "Home," he sighs, his lips grazing the bottom of my neck, next to my shoulder. I feel his stubble against my cheek as he softly brushes his lips up the right side of my throat. "You are home," he breathes, his hand traveling higher and higher.

I bite my lip in anticipation, not knowing what's to come. His tongue dances along my skin, making me tremble. One hand tangles in my hair, the other reaches the edge of my panties, his fingers teasingly close, but not close enough. My chest rises and falls as his open mouth presses against my ear. "I think about being inside you," he says huskily.

The hair on the back of my neck stands up, and warmth pools

between my legs. "You do?" I ask, shivering. *Please don't stop touching me.* I'm in desperate need for his fingers to move.

His lips hover over mine. "Of course I do." He kisses the corner of my mouth then seeks my eyes for permission. One of his hands slides deep into my hair, and he leans in. "I think about the taste of your lips." Starting with a soft peck before he tenderly sucks my bottom lip into his mouth, he then gives the top the same attention. I wrap my arms around his neck, and he cages me in, licking the seam. I open on a whimper, giving and taking all he offers. "The softness of your skin," he breathes against me. His hands roam over my butt, squeezing roughly while he claims my mouth with his wet tongue.

I lift my hips involuntarily, needing to feel him against me. "Your body shaking beneath me." His words ignite a fire inside me. I release a throaty moan, eagerly kissing him back with everything I have. Both of us are panting. "Do you feel what you're doing to me?" he hisses, pressing his hardness against me, closing his eyes. "With those sexy little sounds you make." His lips part, and his eyes pierce into mine. "I think about those, too." His voice nearly cracks.

He reaches for the hem of my shirt, and I help him take it off, wrapping my legs around him. He lifts me off the counter and carries me over to the bed, greedily kissing my mouth before laying me down. I cross my arms over my chest, as his thumbs flick at his waistband, and his jeans fall to the ground.

He crawls on the bed beside me. I wish I'd put on a sexier pair of panties—something silky with a little lace. Instead they're plain, pink cotton. I'm feeling a little insecure. He could easily be paid to model those black boxer briefs he's wearing; of course, he could model anything.

His eyes are hooded as he runs his hand from my shoulder

down to my hip, watching his movement the whole way, as if waiting for something to happen. My skin trembles from the contact. "Don't cover yourself. You're perfect." He peers down on me. "I love watching your body react to me." He presses a soft kiss against my forehead, then temple, and cheek.

I meet his mouth and kiss him tenderly. Fear overtakes me, and my mind begins to wonder how much this is actually going to hurt. I'm about to have sex with Luke Ryann. Just thinking about it makes me nervous, but excited at the same time.

He brushes my hair off my shoulder, peppering kisses across my jawline, down my neck. "What are you thinking about?" he asks quietly. My cheeks flush in embarrassment. I hesitate on whether or not I should tell him the truth.

"I know this is hard for you. Take your time." I swear I feel him smile against my skin, like he already knows. His fingers dance along my collarbone in light, feathery touches. It's calming and turns me on at the same time.

I swallow and close my eyes. "I was thinking about you being inside me." Why was it so hard to get that out? When I'm able to look at him, he's patiently waiting for me to continue. So I do. "Wondering how much it's going to hurt, and if I'm going to like it." I stare at his chest. It's hard to look directly into his eyes after being so vulnerable.

Leaning in, he kisses me. "Coming from the girl who's afraid to say *penis*, I'm surprised you admitted that." His mouth rises at the corners. "I'm proud of you."

Timidly, I grin back before my eyes awkwardly fall to said penis, which is erect.

"It's natural for you to be scared, Reese, but you need to be ready. You don't want to regret it."

"I promise. I'm as ready as I'll ever be."

He scrunches his brows, brushing his thumb along my quivering lip. "Is that why you're trembling?" He can't hide the desire in his eyes. It's there. I can see it.

Sure, I'm scared, but more than anything I'm excited. I cup his face, meeting his gaze. "I'm trembling because I want this … I want you, Luke."

His jaw clenches beneath my hand. It takes a minute to work this over in his head before his fingers run over my skin, and his eyes peer into mine. "Do you want me to touch you?"

My pulse picks up. The sound of his husky voice alone is enough to get me worked up. Unable to look away from him, I nod. His hand hovers over my breast, and he shakes his head back and forth, still staring into my eyes. I feel the warmth before he even touches me. "Say it," he whispers. Chills run up and down my spine. "There's nothing to be embarrassed about. Tell me what you want."

"I want you to touch me," I whimper.

His gaze falls to my breast, then he cups it. "Right here?" He asks, slowly brushing his thumb across the sensitive peak. I cry out in pleasure, and he swallows it down with a deep, erotic kiss, moving his thumb back and forth. He does this for a while, switching from my mouth back to my neck, then releasing me.

He slides down my body, pressing the ridges of his abs and chest firmly against me, then his eyes lift to mine. His lips enclose over my other breast, and he repeats the motion with his tongue that he had just done with his fingers. "Do you like my mouth on you?"

My legs tremble beneath him, and I tug on his hair. "Yes! Please Luke, I need you," I gasp.

His fingers travel down my stomach, then his mouth reaches for mine. "Need me to what?" he asks, our lips less than an inch apart from each other. His eyes are filled with want.

I'm too embarrassed to say it. Instead, I run my hands over his chest, down the ridges of his abs, following his pattern—hoping that'll be enough of a hint—but he grabs my wrist and stretches it above my head. "Uh uh uh, you're making this harder than it has to be." Doing the same with my other wrist, he's gripping them both in one hand. I watch as his tattoos flex above me. It's incredibly sexy.

"I want to touch you," I pant, feeling my chest rise and fall with his. "Let me."

He plants a kiss on my mouth, pressing our foreheads together. His hand dips between my thighs, and his thumb grazes over my panties. I throw back my head and whimper when his fingers slip inside, and he touches my most sensitive part.

Rubbing his nose against mine, his breathing is heavy. "Look at me," he commands. Self-consciously, I do what he says. His eyes burn into me. "The first time I push inside you, I want to look into those beautiful eyes." He licks his lips. "I'll start off slow and gentle … and I won't change the pace until you beg me."

My eyes roll back, and I moan at the sensation his fingers are bringing. "Keep them open," he whispers, releasing my wrists. Gripping my thigh, then placing it over his shoulder, he kisses me fiercely. A fire builds within me.

I grab the back of his head to pull him closer while I delve deep into his mouth. I can't seem to bring him close enough. I will never tire of being underneath him, above him—anywhere he is.

"Luke," I sigh uncontrollably in a voice that isn't mine.

"Am I hurting you?" His thumb gently brushes my cheek.

"No," I pant. "Don't stop!"

His lips graze my ear. "When your body gets used to me, the

pain will subside." He kisses my mouth. "You'll tell me whether you want it fast or slow." His movements match his words. "Gentle or hard, and how deep you want me to go." My chest arches toward the ceiling, and my vision blurs with flashes of light. He licks the side of my neck as my toes curl and my entire body shatters around him. When I cry out, he covers my mouth with one of his hands. The other continues to move until the final tremor escapes me.

I come down from my high, and he releases me, giving me a soft peck on the lips then my cheek before he climbs off the bed.

"What are you doing?" I ask, still catching my breath.

His eyes fall to his erection. He tugs on his hair, then his mouth curves into a devilish smirk. "I need to take care of something," he says, tipping his head toward the shower. "It shouldn't take long."

"Don't you dare," I tell him.

He raises his brows, and I point to his dick.

"I want to take care of you," I say softly. "Please, teach me. It's only fair."

His eyes glaze over, and he makes his way back to bed. A sexy grin crawls across his face. "How can I say no to that?" he replies, sitting down beside me. He takes my hand, and guides me to helping him gain his own release.

My eyes are heavy, and I'm trying my best not to fall asleep, but I can feel myself fading fast. "Why didn't we?" I ask him, laying my head on his chest. I told him I was ready and thought he felt the same.

He sighs. "I'm leaving in the morning. It'd be selfish of me. Is that what you imagined for your first time?" He kisses the top of my head. "To wake up alone?"

I frown thinking about it. "Not exactly."

"Besides, we wouldn't have enough time for what I have planned for you."

I lift my chin and fight back a giddy smile. "Really?"

"Yeah," he says softly, looking down on me with gentle eyes.

What he's saying makes sense. "You're probably right," I murmur. "I'm going to have a hard enough time with you leaving." Sex will just complicate things that much more.

# 20

## Luke

"You look like hell." I flick my eyes away shortly after noticing a small smile form on Andrew's lips. We act like we're looking for groceries, walking down an aisle at a local grocery store in North Phoenix. He's bearded with his hair grown out. Each time I see him he's harder to recognize. I'm not sure what his deal is, but very few people can pull this look off, and he's not one of them.

"That's the idea," he mumbles quietly. "You don't look any better," he adds, eyeing my banged up face. I glance at him sideways, grab a bag of pretzels, and toss them into the cart. It's good to see him again. A crease forms between his brows, as he asks, "How you holding up?"

"What kind of question is that?"

"Right," he murmurs.

"Give me something to hang on to. Tell me we're close." I tug on my hair. "I'm losing my *mind*, Andrew."

He holds out his hands. "We're working on getting you out of there, and it's going to happen soon. I've told you before, this is hard for me, too. You're not alone in this, but you need to be patient."

"Patient?" My eyebrows shoot up. "I'm participating in drug deals while these bastards do away with whomever they please! No one intervenes. How can that be legal?" I hiss through my teeth. "Do you have any idea what it's like to have these things on your conscience?" Pointing to my chest, I add, "I was ordered to kill a couple of kids last night while some filthy fuck was raping their mother in the other room. Is that not enough evidence? What the hell is wrong with this country?"

A mix of pity and understanding crosses his face. "You're not one of them," he says. "You never will be."

I close my eyes and exhale. "I wanted to pull the trigger, Andrew. That's what scares me the most. I wanted him dead."

"That family's safe, because of you." He pauses. "And the children have their mother. You did what you had to do."

An elderly man walks down the aisle, whistling a happy tune. We back away, pretending to browse again.

"Did Glenn buy your story?" Andrew asks, turning the corner as we move on to the next aisle.

"He's hard to read … always has been," I say, dropping two boxes of mac-n- cheese into the cart. "I guess we'll find out when I get back."

We put together a story blaming Samuel's wife for Gage's murder. I was "taking care" of the kids when the gun went off, assuming Gage had shot her. I hadn't expected to find her alive, standing over his body, a gun in her hand. I shot her before she could react, burned the bodies, and went back to clean up the evidence. It was an all-night affair.

He furrows his brows. "If you sense they're suspicious, contact me."

"If I don't have a bullet in my head by then," I answer flatly.

Scratching his bearded chin, he continues. "This isn't the time to joke. You're in dangerous territory, and not just with your father."

I pause. "You think I don't know that? They're using me as a pawn. Fuck, I'm dead already!"

A woman rushes by, pushing a cart. Her expression says she heard me, and I'm guessing I scared her.

"Sorry," I say. She smiles politely then scurries away. I flick my eyes back to Andrew.

He's watching me with pursed lips. "You going to give up?"

I straighten my shoulders. "Hell no. I'll fight to the finish." My hands automatically clench into fists.

He nods slowly. "They still checking you for a wire or weapon?"

"They've let up a little," I say, scratching my head. "Not enough to take a chance. If they catch me, it would be the end."

His mouth opens then closes, and his gaze falls to the ground. He has something to say, but he's just not spitting it out. "Thank you … for protecting her." His eyes lift to mine, and they're filled with emotion. "Remind yourself why you're doing this, when things get unbearable. Maybe that'll help."

I swallow the lump in my throat. "I remind myself every day—a thousand times a day." It's the only way I get through it.

His forehead wrinkles. "Where'd you end up last night? Did you sleep?"

He's not going to like my answer. I hesitate, meeting his eyes.

He sees it on my face. "You saw her."

"I had to. I couldn't leave things the way they were. I needed to see her … talk to her …" *Tell her I love her.*

"Are you sure you weren't followed? Not the best decision on your part."

I shake my head. "I wouldn't have stepped near her if that

were the case. No. Nobody followed me."

He slowly bobs his head up and down, eyeing me curiously. "Do you love her?"

How could he ask that? "Absolutely, I do." I lift my chin. "She means everything to me. She's my light in the darkness. That woman will be the death of me; I guarantee it."

Andrew flinches. "Let's hope not." He grabs a twelve pack of Coke and sets it in his cart. "It's good you saw her," he says, squeezing my shoulder. "Now that you have some competition, it's better she knows how you feel."

My brows pinch together. "Wait, repeat that?"

"Which part?"

"The part about competition." My blood boils, and my head feels ready to explode.

He backs away a few steps, rubbing his forehead. "I thought you knew."

*I don't think so. You told me for a reason.* "Cut the crap. Who is he?" I feel like I was sucker punched in the gut.

Waving a hand, he says, "Some neighbor friend, but you're the one she's in love with. I've seen it on her face whenever we bring you up."

Neighbor friend … the preppy douchebag who pays me rent. "How long?" My jaw clenches. I need to hit something. I raise my fist, but there are kids close to thirty feet away.

"A few months. They were supposed to have dinner last night actually. We'd met for coffee, and she mentioned it. She referred to him as a 'friend,' though I'm sure he's holding out for more," he adds, lowering his voice. "Anyway, let's not make a big deal out of it. You hadn't gotten to her yet. I assume things are patched up between you two?"

Why the hell didn't she say anything? What's she hiding?

That prick's wanted to bang her since the moment he laid eyes on her. I don't trust him. I saw the way he looked at her. Friends … yeah right! I press my lips into a tight line.

"Are you with me?"

Blinking out of my thoughts, I say, "Yeah, you just blindsided me, but I'm with you."

"Good." He grins. "Now use that jealousy and determination to stay alive."

# 11

## Reese

I know that if I open my eyes, the space beside me will be empty. So I wait a little longer while my mind sifts through our night together—Luke lying over me, the intensity in his gaze, the desire I'd seen on his face. The thought of it makes me grin. *Luke Ryann was the first man to touch me.* He made me feel beautiful and adored. And the words that he spoke … don't even get me started. I *loved* it. I love him. I wonder what sex is going to be like. *Ugh.* I don't want to wait anymore. I know it's going to be amazing.

I reach across the bed wondering if it's still warm, but my hand meets a mass of curly hair. My eyes fling open, and I suck in some air. "How many times are you going to creep up on me like that?" I'm staring at a beautiful set of teeth that belong to my smiling best friend. She holds a calla lilly in her hand and brings it to her nose.

"You've been a bad little girl." She passes it to me. "This is for you. Do you know how hard it was to keep Logan from breaking down your door last night?" My cheeks heat instantly. I didn't realize we were that loud. "He thought you were getting it on with Sean." Her brows lift. "What a relief it was for him to bump into Luke this morning, holding a vase filled with three dozen of these."

She sits up and folds her legs behind her. "I've been watching you sleep for twenty minutes. I can't wait any longer. Tell me everything."

"You guys heard us?" I cover my face with my hands, attempting to hide my blush.

"Mostly you," she giggles, and it's then I notice she's still wearing her jammies.

"What time is it?" The clock on my nightstand reads just past seven. Gia's normally asleep right now, and she likes to get ready as soon as she's up. I groan and place a pillow over my face. Luke and I were up late, and I have to work in a few hours.

"I know it's early, but after Logan woke me with the news, I couldn't go back to sleep."

"Honestly? He couldn't wait a little longer?"

She grabs the pillow and tosses it away. "After the fight we had last night?" she says, waving her hand. "Pshht, he couldn't wait to rub it in my face. He always needs to be right."

"I hope he didn't say anything."

"You mean about Sean?" She shakes her head. "Nope. I asked him. He said Luke has enough to worry about, and he'd tell him later when he's back for good."

I groan. "He makes it sound *way* worse than it is."

"Guys don't believe in platonic relationships with the opposite sex."

I lift up my head. "Guys or Logan?"

"Most guys I think. It's hard to understand because we don't have penises." She pulls her hair into a high ponytail. "So what's the explanation? Where has he been?"

I purse my lips then climb off the bed. I can't explain this without looking like a fool. I wish she hadn't asked.

"Uh oh … he didn't tell you." She frowns, not making me feel better.

"I trust him. That should be all that matters, right?" I grab a pair of yoga pants and a pink tank to match then place them on top of the bed.

It takes her a minute to say anything. "I just don't want to see you hurt. I like Luke, but I don't understand the secrets. It worries me." She makes a face like she's waiting for my wrath, but I know she means well.

"Do you trust my judgment?" I ask, lifting my brows. "Are you worried that I've become sort of pushover? Be honest. I want to know."

"No, it's not that," she lies. Furrowing her brows, she continues, "Just promise that you'll be careful." She climbs off my bed and squeezes my hand. "I know you really care about him."

"I do." I squeeze hers back then head to the shower, turning it on. I appreciate her advice, but I'm going to go with my heart on this one. A beautiful vase of lilies sits on the counter. A smile spreads across my lips, remembering all that happened right in their very spot. He lost control, and I'd enjoyed every second of it. "So he bought me my favorite flowers, huh?" I scurry over and inhale them, closing my eyes.

"Aren't they gorgeous?" she asks, tinkering with the large red ribbon that's wrapped around the vase. Her tone is light, which changes the mood a little, and for that I'm glad.

"I wish I'd seen him walk in with them." I was out of it when he kissed me goodbye this morning. I stayed awake as long as I was able to keep my eyes open. I wanted to savor the time we had, and I know he'd done the same. I'm not sure which of us fell asleep first.

"And you didn't even have to screw him to get them."

"Says who?" I look at her surprised, and she grins.

"Says who do you think? The first thing Logan did when he saw him was congratulate him."

My mouth drops open, and I roll my eyes. "What'd Luke say?"

"That it didn't happen … told Logan he had it wrong." She shrugs.

I picture Logan with his hand in the air, motioning a high-five like he's still in high school. I lick my lips. "It wasn't the right time. You know … with Luke leaving again. Things are complicated enough."

She nods. "Yeah, I agree …" Silence. "Anyway, I'll let you shower. Are you working today?"

I start peeling off my clothes. "I've got to be there in a few hours. I think I slept less than that."

She yawns. "Sucks to be you. I'm going back to bed. See you later."

I'm on my way to work and decide to phone my mother for the umpteenth time. This is the longest stretch we've gone without talking, and I'm beginning to worry.

"Hello?"

It takes a moment to register she's answered.

"Mom?"

"Reese. Hi baby," she coos in a motherly voice. I've never understood why she uses it. She isn't the motherly type. "I haven't heard from you in forever. Where have you been, honey?"

My brows shoot up. "Where have *I* been? Where have *you* been?" My mother's crazy. "I've been trying to get ahold of you for three weeks. Have you checked your messages lately?"

"Yeah, I've checked them. I don't recall getting any messages from you, and I've been here. *Tim!*" she shouts, her voice muffled through the phone. "Tell Reese I've been here for the past three weeks. She says she's left messages."

I'm not arguing about whether or not she was there, and I don't want to waste this call on Tim.

"She's been right here," he says in the background.

"Tell her I haven't gotten any messages," she whisper yells at him.

"She hasn't gotten messages."

I roll my eyes. Whatever, I don't care. I'm just glad she's okay.

"I was on my way to work and wanted to check on you. I miss you, Mom," I say, pulling into the parking lot. I only have a few minutes to spare.

"We've been busy, busy, busy!" she squeals. "Tim and I are almost settled in. We've painted walls, hung decorations. We still have a little unpacking ahead of us. But we're making plenty of progress," she adds with relief in her voice. "I can send you pictures if you'd like?"

I smile. "I'd love that. I'm glad you're doing well." And I mean it. She sounds happy, which almost makes me teary eyed.

"We are, Reese. We love it here. With lakes, ponds, and trees wherever you go. There's nothing but green. North Carolina is definitely different from Phoenix," she murmurs. "You'll have to see it sometime."

"Maybe I will." I spot a few students walking toward the entrance. I get out of my car, locking it up. "It sounds beautiful. I'm really happy for you."

"It is, honey. How are things over there? Have you talked to your father lately?"

"I have ... he's doing really well," I say, scurrying ahead toward the double doors. "Listen, I'm at work so I have to let you go. It was good to hear your voice, Mom." I wave to Pam, standing behind the counter with a brilliant smile on her face.

"It's good to hear from you, too, baby. I'll talk to you later."

"I love you." There's a click on the other end, so I put the phone away and shove my purse in the cabinet. For the first time in my life, I'm beginning to think my mother's going to be okay.

We're in a new season, and this is a brand new class—my largest group yet. We start out by teaching simple basics in self-defense—a video the first week, then the next we go over and review. It's always best to keep a situation from getting physical, if possible. Sometimes it's not, though, so I teach them how to protect themselves if that situation arises. There couldn't be a more fulfilling job for me.

"Okay kids. That's it for this week. You all did great!" I smile, meeting each of their eyes. Two of them simultaneously raise their hands.

I point to the shorter girl standing to my left—surprised she has a question. She's been abnormally quiet since we've started. I think her name is Erica.

"When are you going to teach us the good stuff?" she asks shyly.

"Very soon," I tell her. "Since we're only in our second class, you're learning the basics. I'm sure some of you already know most of them, but you'd be surprised by how many don't," I say, placing my hands on my hips. "Once I see that you have them down, we'll move on to the rest. How's that sound?" I ask, raising my brows.

She grins, seeming pleased by my answer, a hint of pink showing on her cheeks. Some of the girls cheer around me. This time we have a boy in class, but only one. I can see he enjoys the attention he's getting; the girls seem to love him.

The second girl lowers her hand. "Did you have a question?"

"You answered it." She smiles.

"Okay then, anyone else have a question?" I ask, clasping my hands together. "All right, class is over." I wave. "Next week is spring break, so I'll see you all in a couple of weeks."

# 12
## Luke

Wrapping a towel around my waist, I make my way to the door. Chance's ears are pulled back, and he's baring his teeth. "Hold up, buddy." Grabbing his collar, I peer through the peephole. My father and Rachelle stand on the other side. "We've got company," I tell him, unlocking the door. I have to force him back when I open it—he's a good judge of character.

"Wasn't expecting company," I say, gesturing them inside. "Let me throw something on real quick." I'd gotten back from Phoenix a couple of hours ago and just stepped out of the shower.

Glenn treads toward the couch, hesitantly taking a seat. "That isn't necessary. I won't be long." He watches Chance, who's fierce and ready to attack him. I'm unable to let him go.

*Good job, buddy.*

Rachelle chooses the recliner, crossing her legs back and forth. She eyes me under lowered lashes. "Do you always answer the door half-naked?"

"Why are you here?" I ask my father, ignoring Rachelle.

His gaze moves from me to the dog, then his hand rests on his gun.

"Hold on a minute." I put Chance outside, set out some water, then shut the door, striding back into the room.

This seems to have relaxed him. "I don't think he likes me very much."

"Me neither." I rake a hand through my wet hair. "Let's start over. Why are you here?"

"You had a rough night," he says like this concerns him. "I came here to check on you … to let you know how proud I am."

My gaze falls to the ground. "I'm not going to lie to you. It was tough, but like you've said, 'business is business.' It had to be done. And sorry about Gage." *Don't be an idiot. He knows you hated him.* "Actually, I'm not. I hated the guy."

Glenn laughs out loud—unexpectedly. There's a gleam in his eyes. "He was a bit of a pest. Wasn't he?" he says, framing his chin with his finger and thumb before Rachelle and I are joining in the laughter. It feels fifty shades of crazy, but I play the part.

A moment later I lean against the wall and cross my arms. Glenn stands up and walks over, handing me a nine-mil. "It's yours. You've earned it." He holds my stare—like he's searching for some sort of father and son connection.

I swallow the bile crawling up my throat and examine the gun. "'Bout time."

"Thought you'd like that," he says, giving a single nod. "Maybe it'll relieve some of the tension."

"I'm sure it'll help," I mumble back.

He smirks, running a finger across his lips. "There's one more gift, but unfortunately it's just a loaner. I'll need it back tomorrow."

Still playing with the gun, I say, "Yeah, okay." I set it down to give him my full attention. "What is it?"

He clasps his hands behind his back. "Rachelle, do me the honors. Tell him what it is."

Her eyes slowly rake over me before she purses her lips and says, "Me." Crossing her other leg, she adds, "I'm your gift."

I let that settle in. "This is a joke, right?" Holding out a hand, I gesture. "No offense. " I chance a glance at my father. "You two aren't together?" I cock a brow, pointing back and forth between them.

He chuckles, patting me on the back. "Ah son, you amuse me. She's an escort." He tilts his head. "You ever been with an escort?" he asks, watching me curiously.

"I've never needed an escort." If I refuse her, he'll be suspicious—maybe think I'm still hung up on Reese. "She any good?" I walk toward her, then lift her chin to get a better look at her face. She licks her lips, expecting me to kiss her, but I hold back. *She wants this.*

"I'll let you be the judge of that." His eyes sparkle. "Don't have *too* much fun. It's just for the night. I have a meeting to attend." He looks at his watch. "Tomorrow there's a potential business partner I'd like you to meet. In the meantime, enjoy your night off."

My eyes flick to Rachelle. She watches me with hooded eyes. This could be one of his ploys—to see if I'd go through with it. With him it's hard to tell. "I'm sure I will. Thanks for the gift." I grin. "I hope she can handle me," I say, walking him to the door. "It's been a long time."

"You have no idea what I can handle," she replies seductively.

I glance over my shoulder, and she winks.

"We'll see about that, sweetheart."

"Tomorrow then," my father says, eyes moving to Rachelle. "Let me know when you contact your friend."

"I'll call you," she answers.

I look from one to the other. "Friend?"

He waves it off. "She can fill you in tonight if you're curious … guns," he sighs. "Anyway, I must get going."

Gripping the doorframe, I ask, "Is there a time you want me to have her back?"

He pauses. "That's entirely up to you, son. We'll figure it out tomorrow. I'll be at the shop."

"See you then."

I close the door and lock it before treading to the back to let Chance in. He races through the kitchen and into the next room, sniffing the area where my father sat. "He's gone, buddy," I tell him. He sniffs around some more then raises his leg. "Chance! Don't even think about pissing on my couch!" Giving me the sad eyes, he lies down.

Rachelle giggles across from him. "He's a beautiful shepherd."

"Yes he is," I reply.

"Looks like he has it out for Glenn."

"He does."

"Why do you think that is?" She stands up, stepping closer. I can smell her perfume.

"Not really sure. Why don't you ask him?" I say, flicking my eyes to Chance. "I'm going to put something on." Leaving her there, I make my way to my room, slamming the door behind me, then quickly putting on some clothes. I rest my hands on the dresser, hanging my head in defeat. I have no idea what to do with this woman.

I hear Chance scratch at the door. I let him in, and he jumps on the bed and stares at me. "What? You were ready to piss on my couch." I scratch behind his ears. "You don't like the girl?" He tilts his head. "Trust me. I didn't invite her." I've officially lost it. I'm explaining myself to a dog.

"Now that's a lie," Rachelle interrupts, standing in the

doorway. Her arms are folded, and one of her brows is arched high—like she's offended.

I rub the space between my brows. "Don't waste your time, sweetheart." Walking into my closet, I grab a shirt and the smallest pair of shorts I own. "I'm not interested in what you're offering," I say, tossing them to her. They hit her in the chest and fall to the ground. "And put on some clothes." She's wearing a very short skirt with stripper heels. Her tank top is at least three sizes too small. She looks trashy.

"Figured you were all talk." She starts taking off her shirt.

I walk out of the room. "You can sleep in here tonight. I'm taking the couch." Chance follows behind me.

"You sure you want to sleep alone?" she asks, coming out of my room a moment later.

I sit in the lazy boy and flip on the television, wondering how, a girl like her ended up in this situation. She's young and attractive, yet she's prancing around a man who's old enough to be her father.

She takes a spot on the couch. "What? Why are you looking at me like that?" she asks insecurely.

I wonder how much he's paying her. "Is it the money?"

"Is *what* the money?" She's feigning stupid, but I see through it.

"Don't give me that shit," I say, looking at her pointedly. "Are you doing this for the money, or is it more than that? Do you owe him for something?"

"I don't know what you mean," she says. "I'm an escort. Of course it's for the money."

"Are there different fees for different services?"

"Yes."

"So what's my old man pay to nail you and pass you around?

Just curious."

Her eyes fall to the floor. "I ..."

"Don't you think that's messed up? Is it really worth the money?"

Lifting her chin defiantly, she says, "Sometimes we have to suck it up and do things we may not like to do. Don't you agree?"

I snort. "Not what *you* do."

"You've never been with a hooker?"

I grin. "That all depends on your definition of hooker. Have I ever paid for sex? No."

"I find that hard to believe," she murmurs under her breath.

"Why pay for sex when I can have it for free?" I lean forward, resting my elbows on my knees. "You're wrong, sweetheart."

"Defensive, aren't we?" She arches a brow. "You think you're the only one who has them fooled?"

"Quit speaking in code and spit it out. Enough of this back and forth shit. Just say what you want to say."

"I know everything, Luke."

I cock a brow. "You saying you're some kind of psychic?"

"Tell me the real reason why you're here—about the fire that killed your mother."

My blood runs cold, and I scrutinize her with my gaze. She must have good reason to bring up my mother. "How about you tell me, Rachelle, or is Rachelle even your name?" I tilt my head. "Are you a cop? A fed disguised as a hooker?"

She clears her throat, fidgeting on the couch. "An escort, remember? And yes, I'm working undercover, so you can spare me the motivational speech about my choices."

"What do you know about my mother?" I ask calmly, wanting to get to the point, even though I'm far from calm.

"If I do, are you going to be nice?"

"Fuck nice! Tell me what you know!"

Her eyes widen. "You think you can keep that temper in check when you're facing your father tomorrow?"

My hands clench into fists. I grab the remote and turn off the television. "He did it, didn't he?"

"The night your father introduced us, you mentioned your mother," she replies softly, tucking her hair behind her ear. "I asked him about it later." She pauses. "He said your mother had threatened to turn him in if he took you along on a deal he'd been planning. There was a lot of money involved. Drug money," she confirms.

"Go on," I say, gesturing her to continue.

"He said it wasn't worth the chance. He told Valdez about her warning. Together, they decided to take care of her."

I blow out a breath then lean back in my chair. "Valdez." Of course. It all makes sense—everything she said. Closing my eyes, I rub the space between them.

Gentle hands rest on my shoulders. "You're right to go after him," she murmurs, as her fingers start to massage me.

"Why would he tell you this?" I'd be stupid to trust her. She's just a stranger claiming to work for the FBI. Maybe she does … maybe she doesn't. How am I to really know?

Her hands still for a second, and then she's massaging again. "A warning." Bringing her head down close to my face, she adds, "To scare me into keeping my mouth shut." Her eyes move to my lips. She wants me and doesn't care to hide it. "Whether you believe it or not, I'm on your side." She smiles. "You can trust me."

I jerk out of my chair. "I'm going out." Making my way to my room, I shut the door behind me and reach for my phone. The call to Andrew goes unanswered. I pocket the phone in my jeans and grab the keys to the Harley.

"I'll go with you," she announces when I walk past her.

Shaking my head, I tell her, "Stay here. I need to be alone." My eyes lift to hers.

She frowns disappointedly. "Just don't do anything stupid."

I tap the doorframe. "I'll try not to." I pause, looking for something else to say. "Anyway, thanks … for telling me about my mother." I don't wait for a response. Instead, I shut the door.

# 13

## Luke

I stopped at a Circle K to pick up a twelve-pack after roaming the streets for about an hour. Being away from Reese, and the stress of what I'm living day to day, is driving me to drink—helps me forget how miserable I am.

I hope she liked the flowers. If she felt anything like I did when she woke up, she needed them. It killed me to leave her there—her hair sprawled out on the pillow, looking beautiful in my shirt, and even more so when she was out of it. It took all my restraint not to take her right then and there. I couldn't do it—not without her knowing the truth, not until this is over. She deserves that and so much more.

I wish she'd told me about the preppy neighbor. My mind runs rampant with thoughts of him wiping away her tears, comforting her, touching her body. I cringe as I pull up the driveway, staring at my house.

When I step inside, Rachelle's curled up on the couch, in the same place where I left her. I imagine her as somebody else with big green eyes then flick my gaze to the TV. That alien movie with the tall blonde chick, the one who used to be a model, is on. I forget what it's called.

"Feeling better?" she asks, turning down the volume.

I make my way to the kitchen and place the beer in the fridge then pop open a bottle. "Sure," I tell her, striding toward the lazy boy.

"You want to talk?"

"Nope." I take a seat without casting a glance in her direction. She wants my attention, and for some reason, it fuels my desire to be more of a dick.

"You got enough to share?"

Stretching my arms back, I kick my feet up on the footstool and gesture her toward the kitchen. "Yep."

"What's with the attitude?" she huffs, getting off the couch. "I'm here to help you."

"I didn't ask for your help," I tell her, keeping my gaze on the screen.

"*No*, but you need it."

I watch the actress shift out of her human form, pinning down a dude as she turns him. "What's this movie called again?" I ask, glancing at Rachelle.

Her lips are pursed. She swings her hair over her shoulder. "Are we going to talk about this, or are you going to ignore me the rest of the night?"

I cock a brow. "Talk?" Tipping my beer toward the TV, I add, "Thought we were watching a movie."

"Okay." She nods. "No biggie. I just figured you'd be interested in learning about the progress we're making on the case."

She's right; I'm interested. "You going to tell me about it?"

"You going to stop being a dick?"

I rub my chin. "That all depends on how much you tell me."

"Unfortunately, it doesn't work that way."

"How 'bout you tell me what you want, and we'll go from

there."

She straightens her shoulders. "Open up a little. Talk to me. It's all I ask. We don't have to be best buds or anything," she says, licking her lips. "Believe it or not, we're going to need each other."

*I don't think so.* "You want me to talk to you," I confirm, raising my brows.

"Yeah."

After pondering it, I tell her, "Fair enough. I'll talk to you." But I'm not giving her anything important.

"Good." She grins. "You know that 'friend' of mine your father had mentioned earlier?"

"Earlier today when he dropped you off?" I raise my brows.

"Yeah. We're meeting tomorrow. He's supposed to bring a small supply of AK47s. I told your father I had someone who could hook him up—someone I work with."

"How many guns is he looking to get?"

"One-point-five mil worth."

"Wow."

"Yeah." She grabs a couple more beers, bringing them over. "Anyway, my *friend* is actually an agent ... well, several of them." After handing me a beer, she sits back down. "Tomorrow they'll tell me where to meet them and what to say to Glenn. If all goes well, we'll go from there. Glenn wants to have the samples in his hands before he'll agree to any trade. He's careful that way." She taps on her temple.

"So if this deal goes through, they'll charge him for what? Illegal gun trafficking?"

"Yes."

"And the murder of Samuel?"

"After we charge him for the guns, he'll be interrogated for the murder of Samuel, as well as the conspiracy to commit murder on the rest of his family. We'll also need your testimony."

"That won't be a problem. What about Valdez and the coke?"

"Valdez is another story," she sighs. "From what I hear, it may never go through." She spins her empty bottle on the table. "The kidnapping and murders are enough to put him away for good. He's currently under surveillance. If they move in on him too soon, it'll point directly to you."

"How's that?" I cock a brow.

"You raised a stink about the girl and lost your temper. Knocked out one of his men in one punch. It'll make you look like the rat. It's better they catch him in the act, otherwise you're dead whether they've got him or not."

"When will you know more?" I ask, finishing off my beer, setting the bottle down beside me.

"That all depends," she says, shrugging. "I check in regularly. If they have something, they tell me." Both of us are quiet for a moment until she adds, "Can I ask you a personal question?"

I lean back and rest my head in my hands, glancing at her. "Sure. Knock yourself out."

She closes an eye hesitantly. "Are you gay?"

"Wait, what?" I cough and laugh at the same time.

"Gay," she replies. "For instance, I know I'm attractive," she says, tucking her hair behind her ear. "Most guys would take advantage of an opportunity to be with me. You brush me off. I'm not used to that."

I stare at her a minute. She obviously thinks pretty highly of herself. "I definitely must be gay then," I scoff. "Look, I love women. I'll always love women … just to make that very clear."

"Then I have another question." She tilts her head. "Though I really don't see you as the type."

"What type is that?" Kicking down the footstool, I sit up in my chair.

"The relationship type. Are you committed to someone?"

Meeting her eyes, I answer, "I don't have time for relationships. They never work." I won't mention anything related to Reese. Rachelle goes back to Glenn tomorrow, and I still can't say I trust her, though I'm starting to. She does seem to genuinely want to help.

She frowns. "When was the last time you were with a woman?"

I raise my brows, surprised by her invasiveness.

"What?" Her eyes widen. "It's an honest question." Setting down her drink, she waits for my answer. I'm ready to call it a night.

"I'm going to bed." I stand up, cracking my neck from side to side, avoiding her eyes.

"It's still early," she whines.

"For who?"

"Anyone under sixty. What is it with you?" She folds her legs up on the couch.

"When you talk to your 'friend' about the guns, tell Glenn I'm going with you." Tipping my head toward the hall, I ask, "Final offer … bed or the couch?"

She frowns. "I can't sleep yet. I'm still wide awake."

"Stay up then. If you can't get comfortable, wake me up, and I'll switch you." I stride down the hall into my room, then pull the comforter off of my bed, taking it to her. "In case you get cold, though I doubt you'll need it."

"Thanks, I guess." She flicks her gaze toward the television, crossing her arms in a huff, then I leave her and head off to bed.

# 14

## Reese

"**S**o what's the hurry? What is it that brings us to this emergency coffee meeting?" I tease my dad. He called me up this morning asking if I'd meet him for coffee. He said he needed to talk to me. "To be honest, I thought you'd be bringing a woman—a new love interest perhaps."

His eyes crinkle at the sides. "With this?" he asks, gesturing toward his beard. "I doubt it."

Shaking my head, I reply, "Shave it off then, silly." I sip on my latte and accidentally burn my tongue.

"Personally, I'd rather get to know my daughter again." His words warm my heart. "Which brings me to why we're here." He purses his lips, and his gaze drops to the table.

"Uh oh," I murmur uneasily. "You might as well spit it out instead of making me nervous."

"I'm leaving town for a while, but I wanted to see you before I left. Unfortunately, I won't be making our usual routine." His expression is sad, like he's really going to miss me, and I realize I'm going to miss him too.

"How long?"

"I'm not sure yet … a couple of weeks maybe. A month at the

longest."

"Is it something for work?" He does under the table detective work for a couple of friends on the police department.

"More like an adventure."

My eyes widen. "An adventure, huh? Is this sort of like a mid-life crisis kind of thing?"

"No, nothing like that." He pauses. "It's just something I need to do … something I've been thinking about doing for a while."

"Okay." I nod in understanding, though I'm a little confused. "Do you have a particular place in mind, or is this a spontaneous thing?"

"There are a few places." He takes a small sip of his coffee. "But wherever I end up, it may be hard to get ahold of me." He opens his wallet and pulls out a card. "If there's any kind of trouble while I'm gone, I want you to call this number. He's a friend of mine."

I glance at the card, flipping it over. "I don't get it?" I move my eyes back to him. "FBI? Is that really necessary?"

"Regardless of how you see it, you'll always be my little girl. You can never be too careful." Putting his wallet back into his pocket, he adds, "Just put it away, and say you'll use it if needed. It's just a precaution."

"Okay," I murmur softly, doing what he says before changing the subject. "Oh, I forgot to tell you," I say, scooting closer. "I got ahold of Mom."

His brows lift. "Finally able to reach her, huh? How is she?"

"Better than ever, actually. At least she seemed that way. It was refreshing to hear her so happy."

He pauses, leaning back in his chair. "That's good." Giving a single nod, he continues, "I'm glad to hear that." A flash of jealously appears in his gaze then quickly goes away. I don't think he's ever fully moved on after splitting from my mother.

I probably shouldn't have said anything. "Yeah, me too." I lick my lips, thinking of a way to fill the awkward silence. "So, what are your plans for the day?"

His shoulders straighten. "Nothing until later." Clearing his throat, he asks, "You?"

"None for me either." I sip my coffee. "Would you like to come by, see my place? I have the day off." *Ugh. Why do I sound so nervous?*

A wide grin stretches across his face. "Sure. I thought you'd never ask."

I smile back, and the tension inside me fades. After a few more minutes of talking, we finish our coffees, and he follows me back to my place.

My father's been silent since the moment he stepped inside, focusing on every little detail, from the spacious rooms to the hardware on the doors. I want him to tell me what's going on in that head of his, because the silence is making me paranoid. I can barely stand another second of it.

"Okay, tell me what you're thinking." I chew on my lip.

He turns to me with his hands in his pockets. "I'm impressed. Do you always keep it this clean?"

I sigh in relief. I'd just tidied it up this morning. "Most of the time," I reply. This isn't a lie.

"It's a lot cleaner than the home you grew up in. You definitely didn't get that quality from your mom or me." He chuckles lightheartedly. He's not wrong about that.

"No, I guess not," I murmur.

Heading back toward the living room, his eyes continue appraising the home. "Really, Reese, this is great. I'm happy for you." His approval means more to me than I'd imagined.

"Thank you. I love it here." Stepping into the kitchen, I ask, "Can I get you something to drink? A water, or soda, maybe?"

"I'll take a water if it isn't any trouble."

"Not at all." I grab two bottles out of the fridge, bringing one over to him.

"You said you own this free and clear?"

"Yes, free and clear." Saying the words out loud feels humbling.

"And that's a regular thing for Luke to do? Hand out free homes to beautiful women?" His eyes crinkle at the sides.

It's hard to hold back my grin. "I don't think so."

"No, neither do I," he replies. "Sounds like he really cares for you." He walks over to the couch and takes a seat. "I hope you're making the right decision in moving on," he says, crossing an ankle over his knee.

"Actually …" I sit in the spot beside him, hesitating at first. "I saw him."

His brows shoot up. "You saw him." He watches my face curiously. "Well, how did it go?"

"It was great until he had to leave again." I shrug with a frown, then we both sit back. "One of the hardest parts is explaining it to someone who doesn't understand him. There are a lot of important questions I don't have the answers to, but I feel I need to trust him." I look at my father. "Does that make sense?"

"It does," he murmurs back. "No one else would understand unless they were in your situation. Don't let their reactions get to you." He leans forward. "Do you love him?" His gaze stays with mine.

"Yes. I'm in love with him." Completely. I can't believe I just said that to him.

He nods. "Hold on to him then," he says, patting me on the knee. "Good things come to those who wait." Narrowing his eyes, he adds, "The *other* guy needs to go."

"The other what?" I tilt my head, confused for a second, before it finally registers. "You mean Sean?" I forgot I'd even mentioned him to my father. I think it's cute he remembers and genuinely seams to care.

Waving a hand, he says, "Whoever it was you were talking about the other day," he grumbles. "The neighbor guy."

I laugh. "Sean and I are just friends. And I remember a time when you hated Luke." I point at him.

"No, I never hated the boy." He shakes his head. "I was jealous. He was more of a man than I was — protecting you from me, and others when I wasn't able to do it myself." He grimaces. And there it is: the real reason he's become so fond of Luke. He also blames himself for what happened with Ronald, which is ridiculous.

"You're definitely not the father I knew back then, but you're right. He did protect me."

The door swings open, and we turn our heads as Gia and Logan step inside.

"Well hello, Mr. Johnson," Gia says with a bright smile. My dad stands up, and they meet in the middle, greeting each other with a warm hug.

He places his hands on her shoulders. "Gia, so good to see you again." His eyes lift to Logan's. This must be …"

"Logan." He reaches out a hand, stepping forward.

"That's right," my father says. "I've heard a lot about you."
*No, he hasn't.*

"Uh oh," Logan replies. "From who? Your daughter or Gia?" Logan's eyes flick to mine.

"Both." My father laughs. "You're the one who gives my daughter a hard time."

Logan stutters, and his face turns red.

*Ha! Take that!*

Looking toward me with a twinkle in his eyes, my father adds, "She could use a good teasing every now and then." He winks.

I roll my eyes. "Dad! Don't encourage him."

Logan chuckles beside him. "I like this guy," he tells me.

"Reese was showing me your place. It's a great little set up you have here."

"Thanks!" Gia replies. "We love it."

"That's exactly what she said," he says, referring to me before he sighs. "Well, it's about that time." He glances at me. "I better get going."

"Thanks for stopping by," Gia tells him. "Though I wish we could have had a longer visit." Her brows pinch together.

He nods. "Next time."

"It was nice to meet you, Mr. J—"

I walk my father to the door. "Thanks again for the coffee. Are you leaving tomorrow?" My voice squeaks a little.

"I am," he says lowly, waiting to see if I'll go in for the hug for the first time since we've reunited. He's always the first to reach in, this time holding me tighter. "I love you," he murmurs.

I nod, still unable to say it back, even though I know love him, too. I don't know what's wrong with me—why I can't say it. Logan and Gia aren't helping the awkward moment, standing there and watching us. "Bye Dad. Be safe." There's a lump in my throat while I gently pat him on the back.

"You too."

I hear the emotion in his voice, before he backs away, and I watch him 'til he's gone.

"I like him," Logan says, resting his feet up on the coffee table, facing Gia and me in the kitchen.

"Well, he seems to like you, too," I reply. "It's funny, both of you share the same opinion of Sean, and neither of you are willing to give him a chance."

Logan presses his lips together, raising his brows. "Cool, I like him even more," he retorts. "Don't worry. I'm not going to say 'I told you so.'"

"Thank you for that."

He nods. "You bet."

"Leave her alone," Gia replies as she continues working on her homemade salsa.

"It's okay. I can handle him." I don't need her fighting my battles for me, even though she means well.

"You sure?" She tilts her head.

"Yeah, I'm fine." *I'm not a wounded puppy, Gia,* I want to say, but decide against it.

She smiles. "Your dad's really different," she says, changing the subject. "In a good way, though," she reassures.

"I know. Crazy, isn't it?"

"It is." She pauses, thinking. "Speaking of crazy, what's up with the beard?" she asks, grabbing a handful of tomatoes.

I snort out a laugh. "Believe me, I've asked him. He doesn't give me a straight answer. He knows I hate it."

"I was going to say something about it," Logan adds from the couch. "He hasn't always had it?" He chuckles.

"God no!"

"That's awesome!"

"No, it's not! I told him he should at least trim it up if he ever wants to get back into the dating pool."

Logan shrugs. "Maybe he wants to stay single."

I raise my brows. "It's possible."

"Speaking of single ..." He tips his head toward the window. "How's *Loverboy* handling the news?"

"*Logan*," Gia interrupts, irritated.

"It's fine," I tell her, walking to the couch to sit down beside him.

"He didn't take it well, did he?" he says happily, sipping on his Coke.

I close my eyes and blow out a breath. "I haven't told him yet." When I open them I think he's ready to choke me. "Calm down. We're going out tomorrow. And I plan on telling him then."

"How convenient," he scoffs.

"Look, it isn't that big of a deal. We were never dating."

"According to whom?" he replies harshly. "Don't make me regret not saying anything to Luke," he points. "I did that for you, by the way."

Nice guilt trip. "I won't. I'm going to tell him."

# 15
## Luke

"I'm sorry." I tuck her hair behind her ear, so I can see her beautiful face. "I couldn't sleep."

I want to tell her I came straight from Tucson, that I've been living there the past five months, and tonight, a woman I barely know is sleeping on my couch. There are so many unspoken truths between us, and I want to divulge it all, but decide it's best I keep that information to myself … at least for now. I don't want to upset her any more than I already have.

She doesn't seem bothered that I've showed up at four in the morning. I'm breaking all the rules, but I just couldn't stay away from her. I haven't stopped thinking about the other night. In fact, she's *all* I think about.

"Don't apologize," she murmurs softly. "I haven't been sleeping since you left."

"Are you okay?" I ask, running my thumb along her jawline.

She closes her eyes. "No, Luke. I'm not," she says, hurt evident in her voice.

I did this to her, and I feel like a giant piece of shit. "Then talk to me." I bring her face toward me.

She lifts her gaze to mine with anger in her features. "I want you to make love to me. No more excuses or holding back. This has gone on for far too long."

"You're serious?" My brows shoot up, as my eyes scan her face. "That's what's gotten you upset?" I'm actually relieved.

Biting the center of her lip, she slowly nods. I can tell she's embarrassed.

"Come here." I smile. Picking her up by the waist, I place her over my lap. "If you know this is what you want, then it's yours. I've been ready, Reese." I cup her sweet face, as my heart thumps hard inside my chest.

She smiles; straddling my hips, she leans down to press her mouth against mine. I brush back the dark curtain of hair that tickles my face, gently securing it behind her ear. She pulls away and laughs shyly. "Sorry," she says, her cheeks turning a sexy shade of pink.

I'm just trying to get better access. Those lips are calling for me to kiss them until they're red and swollen. My mouth tips into a grin. "Are you sure you're ready for this?" I scan her face for any apprehension. There are so many things I want to do with her—to her.

"More than anything," she answers. She's glowing, and I feel like the devil corrupting her. The innocence in her green eyes captivates me. Flipping her onto her back, I crawl over her like a predator. Taking her wrists and stretching them above her head, I can see her breasts rise and fall in anticipation; she likes this. Knowing I'm the only one who's gotten her worked up like this makes me feel like the luckiest man alive.

A fire burns in her eyes before she lifts her neck and slams her mouth against mine. "I hate you," she pants, biting down on my lip then licking the sting away. The words catch me by surprise, but this aggressive side is pretty sexy, and I'm harder than ever before. She wants me to take care of her now, and I plan to do that.

Her tongue delves deep inside my mouth. She continues to lick and bite me. Groaning, I want to show her what she's doing to me, so I let go of her wrists, grip her ass with one hand, and grind myself against her. Her head falls back and her lips part. Now it's her turn to moan. "You like this?" I reach for the hem of her shirt, press my lips lightly against hers, then quickly tear it off, exciting her. "You want to play rough, I'll show you rough."

She wraps her legs around me. I slip my tongue into her mouth again, kissing her deeply, then reach down and squeeze one of her breasts. But something isn't right.

"I'll play however you want," she says, tugging me closer, her thighs gripping me tighter. "There's no reason to fight this, if it's what we want." *What?* I pull away, confused, then her eyes change color in front of me, morphing from green into brown as her skin begins to shed. *What the hell?* I try to roll off, but her arms pin me with a force that in no way could be human.

"What are you?" I hiss. Her skin is ridiculously hot.

She tips her head back with a wicked laugh. "Are you afraid?"

*Yeah, I think I am.* I'm sweating profusely. "You're skin ... it's on fire."

I hear a scratching on the door, jerking me awake. It takes a moment to catch my breath. A slow grin slides across my face, and I chuckle quietly. "That was intense." Reese was an alien, and she was terrifying. I realize I'm covered in sweat and reach over to throw off the blanket, but my hand meets a long smooth leg.

I react immediately, pinning her down by her throat. "Why the hell are you in my bed?"

Her eyes widen in excitement.

"Answer me, woman! Tell me why you're here and not on the couch where you should be?"

Finally, looking a little scared, Rachelle gasps, "Let go."

Releasing her, I climb out of bed, not knowing whether to apologize or yell at her again.

"Good morning to you, too," she snaps, pulling the sheet over her head.

I narrow my eyes. "You were supposed to wake me, not cuddle me and shit! Damn!"

She drops the sheet back down to her waist. Her eyes move to my morning wood. "Don't act like you didn't enjoy it, *happy hands.*"

"Happy what?" I ask, pointing to the bed. "Did I touch you?" I tug on my hair. "'Cause if I did, then I'm sorry. If you'd stayed on the couch, I wouldn't need to explain it. I was in the middle of an intense dream."

She yawns. "Blame it on anything you want," she says, running her fingers through the tangles in her hair. "Whatever strokes your ego."

"It has nothing to do with my ego, sweetheart. It's the truth, and you weren't a part of it."

She arches her brows nearly to her hairline. "Really? Then who was this lucky girl?"

"Hell if I know. Some blonde with really big tits." I motion with my hands. "Then you had to come along and ruin it."

Pursing her lips, she's slowly analyzing me. "You're lying," she says.

"You're wasting my time," I reply, grabbing a pillow. "You locked my dog out, by the way," I tell her, making my way to the couch. Chance lies on the floor beside me. I reach down and pat him on the head. "Don't blame me. She did it."

A moment later she's moving about the kitchen, making sure to be extra loud. "What do you have to eat?"

I fluff my pillow and turn on my side. "You have eyes. Use them." Yeah, I'm being a dick. I don't care.

"Some host you are." She searches restlessly through the cabinets, like the nutcase she is.

I lie on my back and stare at the ceiling. "I'm not trying to win any awards, sweetheart."

"It's a good thing," she retorts. "By the way, I need you to take me to pick up my phone. I'm going to find out where we're meeting my guys … for the guns. Then I'll run it through to your dad."

I hope this works and the deal goes smoothly. "Do me a favor. Don't call him that," I tell her, pinching the space between my brows.

"Call who what?"

"My dad."

"Sorry," she says.

Getting off the couch, I stretch my arms back and notice she's only in a shirt—*my shirt*. She must have ditched the shorts last night, before she decided to climb into my bed and wrap her legs around me like a monkey.

"What?" Her lips slowly curve into a smile. "Did I just catch you checking me out?"

*Well shit. Was I? If I was, I sure as hell wasn't meaning to. And now she's biting her lip.*

The last thing I want to do is lead her on. I can't blame the woman for trying. She doesn't know I'm with someone, and therefore thinks I'm available. Avoiding her eyes, I tell her, "I'll be in the shower. You going to put something on?" *Some jeans, shorts, a skirt maybe — something to ease the guilt for whatever I did last night.* Even though I'd never *consciously* touch her.

"Way to change the subject." She pours some cereal into a bowl then fills a glass with water. "Yeah, I've got clothes, but I want to enjoy your shirt a little longer." Taking a long, slow whiff, she grins. "It smells good."

"You can keep it." I'll never wear it again.

"Don't do me any favors," she grumbles. "It's not like I haven't worn a man's shirt before."

"Fine. Don't keep it then." I walk toward my room. Thought I'd be nice for once, since she's helping me out.

"Okay, you talked me into it," she says over my shoulder.

"**L**ook, I want to apologize for being rough with you this morning. I wasn't expecting any company, and whether you believe me or not, I was in the middle of a pretty wild dream. Anyway, I'm sorry," I say, gripping the steering wheel extra tight, as we look for our turn off. I glance over at Rachelle who appears to have dropped her mouth into her lap.

"Well, well, well …" She grins. "You *do* have a heart. Apology accepted."

"Thank you." I nod. "How much farther do we have to go, and do they know I'm coming?"

"It should only be a couple more miles. The last sign we passed said six, and that was a few miles back," she says, checking her phone. "And yes, they know you're coming." They had switched the meeting spot, back when we were at the gas station. We were headed in the opposite direction before they slapped us with the change. I guess the other spot had too many people, and they didn't want to draw any attention.

She sighs. "The sooner we get the guns, the sooner this ordeal will be over. Look! There it is." She points to the exit.

I veer toward the ramp. "You think they're here already?"

"I hope."

"Are you nervous?"

"A little. There's always that chance something could go wrong."

We pull into the rest stop. There's only one other car — a newer black BMW-7 series — and two men are stepping out of it with blank looks on their faces.

"Did they say what car they'd be driving?"

"No, but that's got to be them," she says confidently.

"Are you sure?"

She nods. "They said there'd be two men." They're wearing dark sunglasses and resemble each other.

"Do you recognize them?"

They look to be somewhere in their thirties, black-haired, clean cut, and well-dressed.

"I can't tell yet, but they're looking this way. Pull in there. We'll just load them right into the trunk."

"How much are we loading? You said it's just a sample's worth, correct?" Just as I'm parking the car, I hear a shatter in the back, before bullets are flying over my head. Slamming on the gas, I lie sideways. There's glass all over the backseat, and my headrest just exploded all over me. "Shit! What was that?"

Rachelle panics, crouching down. "I don't know!" Her hands are trembling while she digs into her purse, pulling out a gun.

I spin the car around and speed toward the exit, unable to see over the hood. Bullets are coming at me. More glass shatters on my side. If I'm hit, it's my adrenaline keeping me alive.

"Get us out of here, and try to stay down!" she shouts,

shooting out my window, but she's not really aiming at anything, just protecting herself from the bullets.

Reaching for my gun, I swerve us onto the side road that'll get us back to the highway. I have a split second to check her for injuries. "You okay?"

"I'm fine! Just go!" she tells me, checking over her shoulder.

When I glance in the rearview, I see them a few cars back and press harder on the gas. "Should have gone with the upgrade," I say, switching lanes.

"What?" she asks frantically.

"I said, I should have gone with the upgrade, like a Porsche. The Mustang's a rental."

The shots come again, and I duck down fast.

"Why do you think they're after us?"

I examine the shattered windows, the backseat, the doors, and not a single bullet has hit the passenger side. I watch Rachelle suspiciously. "Are you lying?" Flicking my gaze to the rearview mirror, I add, "Setting me up?"

Her eyes get huge. "What? No! I don't know any more than you at this point!" She once again checks over her shoulder.

Something sharp zips past my ear, and I instantly feel the sting. Bringing my hand up, blood oozes onto my fingers, before I move into the right lane. "You sure? There isn't anything you need to tell me?" I spin around and step on the brake. A semi blocks their view just in time.

"Oh my God, Luke you're hit!"

Grabbing my gun, I wait 'til I get a clear shot of their two front tires, then one by one I blow them out. They swerve to the right, dipping down into the dirt, stirring up a thick cloud of dust. The car flips onto its side. I pop a bullet in the other two tires for the hell of it. "That's what I'm talking about."

"Luke! We need to get you out of here! Shit! Why didn't I charge my phone?" She panics, slipping her gun back into her purse.

Looking behind me toward the wreckage, I know they're both still alive, but they better be hurting.

"Do you need me to drive?"

"It's just a little blood," I say, glancing at her. "It only grazed me."

She leans in to get a better look. "Are you sure? It's more than you think," she says, sounding genuinely scared.

Speeding away from the scene, I tell her, "I'm fine."

"There's *no way* those men are FBI," she replies. "They couldn't be."

I let out a sardonic laugh. "What was your first clue?"

"Who were they? Why would they want us dead?"

"You're the fed. Figure it out."

"We don't know everything," she mumbles. "And sometimes my position makes me last to know certain things."

"Don't worry, sweetheart. They're not after you."

She glances around the car. "I know how this may look," she murmurs. "But truly, I have no idea who those men are. You believe me, don't you?" Her brows pinch together.

"I don't know what I believe."

"Luke."

I grip the steering wheel even tighter than before. "Back at the gas station, who told you to switch locations?"

Unable to meet my eyes, she says, "It was a text. It's not uncommon, and they used the code." She pauses. "Though it was from a number I didn't recognize."

"What code?"

"To authenticate our messages. There's a code we use for

safety reasons …" Her eyes widen. "To prevent incidents like this from happening."

"Then is there some kind of leak?"

She frowns. "God, I hope not, but it's possible." She cringes. "Luke, you're bleeding pretty bad. You sure you're okay?"

"I said I'm fine."

Tilting her head to think, she says, "What if Valdez set this up? Maybe he knows you turned him in?"

"Maybe it was my father. I don't trust him," I reply.

"No." She shakes her head. "That wouldn't make any sense. They'd be after both of us if that were the case. I don't think it was Glenn."

"Guess you better call your *friends* and find out what the hell's going on then." She's the one who got us into this mess in the first place, so she needs to figure it out.

Crossing her arms in a huff, she says, "Stop staring at me like that."

I get off the highway and head to the shop. "You threw us into a warzone over a text. How do you expect me to stare at you?"

"I explained it to you already. It's not uncommon for us to communicate by text. Where are we going?"

"Somewhere where you're safer, which is far away from me."

"It was an honest mistake!"

"I appreciate your honesty, but I've got shit to do."

Her mouth drops. "You have no idea how much you need me. I can help you," she points out.

"Did I ask for your help?" I cock a brow.

"Doesn't matter. You won't make it here without it."

# 16
## Luke

I park the Mustang and get out, slamming the door behind me. I don't bother waiting for Rachelle. She'd been griping about having to pee for the last ten minutes, but I didn't care, telling her she needed to hold it. That just pissed her off. I had one thing on my mind, and that was to find out if Glenn had anything to do with our friendly shooters. She may think differently, but I'm not so sure.

"You don't have to be so cold, you know," she snaps bitterly.

I open the door to the entrance, glancing over my shoulder. She's taking her precious time. "Hurry up already."

She gives me the evil eyes. "You're a real asshole!" Storming past me, she makes her way to the bathroom.

"Blame it on the gunshot wound to the head." I tread to the back.

"Son," my father calls me over the second I push through the door, like he can sense I am here. "There's someone I'd like you to meet. The two of you will be working together."

Right now that's the last thing on my mind. I stride toward my father, fuming. "I need to talk to you. Now," I demand, ignoring the man on my left.

Anger flashes across his features. "Excuse my son for his terrible manners," he murmurs then turns his attention back to me. His gaze drops to the gun I hold firmly in my hand. He smirks. "Am I in trouble? Was the pussy not good enough for you?" Finally bringing his gaze up to my face, he pauses. "Have you been shot?" he asks, noticing the wound on my head. It's hard to tell if he's genuinely concerned or if this is all part of an act, but it's safe to say it's the latter.

"We didn't get the guns," I reply. "Tell me you didn't already know that."

He looks around for Rachelle. "Where is she?"

"The restroom. She wasn't a target. She's shaken up, but she's fine." I turn to acknowledge the stranger, getting the shock of my life when I actually see who is. I blink, reaching out my hand. "Luke Ryann," I say, clearing my throat, erasing the confusion from my expression. What the hell is he doing here? If my father recognizes him, it ruins everything. Why is he taking the risk?

He grips my hand tightly. "Drew." he replies sharply. I get the sense that he's angry, and for whatever reason, his anger's directed at me. "Looks like you were grazed by a bullet." He's focused on the side of my head. "You got lucky this time," he says through his teeth.

Rachelle enters the room, relief flowing through her when she sees my father. She races into his arms.

Andrew flicks his eyes back and forth between us. His brows pinch together.

"Who would do this?" Rachelle asks my father. "I didn't recognize either of them. As soon as we pulled up, they started shooting," she says, nuzzling her head against his chest.

"Are you hurt?" my father asks, looking her over. It's strange to see him care for her when he'd been so quick to hand her over.

Then again, I'll never be able to understand his way of thinking, so why even try?

"No. I'm just a little traumatized. I thought I was going to die," she says, looking toward me. "Luke saved my life."

"They won't bother you anymore," my father replies, stroking her hair affectionately. "I'm assuming you took care of it?" He lifts his brows at me.

Growling, I answer, "I couldn't get a clear shot. They're still alive, if that's what you mean."

"How'd you get away?"

"I blew out their tires and got the hell out of there."

"Luke was shot," Rachelle interrupts. "There was so much blood. I was afraid they'd shoot me next." Her eyes water. "I'm sorry, Luke. I was terrified. I know you wanted them dead," she adds, clinging to my father.

Narrowing my eyes on him, I say, "They changed the meeting spot, last minute." Stepping closer, I continue, "Did you know anything about that? Those men weren't her friends. This was a set up."

"What are you saying, son?" Glenn replies, rubbing his hand up and down Rachelle's back.

"Are you trying to have me killed? 'Cause if you are, be a man and do it yourself!" I shout, spreading my arms.

He glances at Andrew. "Go after my own son? I hadn't realized he thought so low of me," he says, letting out a short laugh, before Andrew's joining in.

I get in Andrew's face. "The fuck *you* laughing at?" Lifting my gun, I cock it. He stands his ground without a flinch, playing his part beautifully.

"That'll be enough!" my father interrupts, the amusement no longer in his eyes. I'm positive I've embarrassed him.

Keeping my gaze on Andrew's, slowly backing away, I get the feeling my father doesn't have a clue who his new friend is, which is good.

"Don't take your bad day out on my guest," my father says. "Can you think of a reason someone would want you dead?"

"I'm not aware of any enemies. I do what I'm told, then I go home."

"Are you sure about that?"

"I'm not sure about anything." I change the subject. "But I'm curious. What'd you hire *him* for?"

"We're partners," he answers, looking at Andrew. "My son's new to the business. You'll have to forgive him."

"I understand," Andrew replies.

"Partners in what?" I glance at both of them.

Gazing at Andrew, he says, "Would you like to tell him?"

He rubs his bearded chin. "How 'bout I show him."

"Fair enough." Glenn turns to Rachelle and says, "You've had an eventful day. I'll get you home. Luke, see Drew out."

Andrew's already headed for the door, glancing over his shoulder. "We'll talk tomorrow, Glenn."

"I'll be in touch," my father tells him, flicking his gaze back to me. "Go home when you're finished. Clean yourself up. And don't forget to show some fucking respect to your elders," he spits. "I need this deal to go through." He's staring at me with disgust in his eyes. "Get out of here. I can't look at you any longer." He tucks Rachelle into his side, kissing the top of her head.

Nearly telling him to fuck off, I decide against it, then make my way through the shop. Andrew leans against a red car parked in the parking lot. When I head over, he opens up the trunk and peers inside.

I stand right beside him. "Are you insane? Is this the reason you got that nappy hair growing out of your face?"

"We need to get you out of here," he replies, glancing at the side of my head. "Have you checked yourself in the mirror lately?"

"I've been a little busy." My eyes fall to the large amount of cocaine inside the trunk. "Shit! Where'd you get all this?"

"I have my sources. Listen," he says, narrowing his eyes. "They're moving in on Valdez."

"Yeah, I know. That woman in there is a fed. She filled me in on some of it."

"She told you that?" he asks, surprised.

"She did. She also knows what I'm up to. What are they charging him with?"

He watches over my shoulder, making sure the coast is clear. "Enough to put him away for good." He frowns.

"Did he … is the little girl?" I'm not able to finish the sentence. I hate that I left her there, tied up and defenseless.

"She's alive, but she's been through a lot, and she's parentless." His brows pinch together. "You mentioned Valdez had something to do with your mother?"

"I'm pretty sure of it." I swallow.

He scans my face. "And the hit on you today. Was it Glenn's doing?"

"It's possible, unless Valdez knows the feds are on to him, and he's getting revenge. Rachelle seems to think that's the case."

"Which is another reason we're getting you out of here."

"You think Glenn knows about it?"

"I'm not sure, but if they're only after you, then Valdez could be going behind his back. After all, you are Glenn's son."

"How'd you get Glenn to trust you?" I tilt my head.

"The DEA has information. They gave me a few names of

their informants, who are high up in the trade." He closes the trunk. "I offered him a deal he couldn't refuse." He shrugs. "He made the call, cancelling what he had going with Valdez shortly after."

"It's a good thing because when word gets out about his arrest, it's going to raise suspicions. Not just with you, but with everyone in your father's circle."

"That includes you," I tell him.

He rubs his chin. "I'm banking on law enforcement intervening before that happens. The deal needs to close tomorrow."

The possibility seems too good to be true. I need to see it to believe it. "Okay, so what do we do?"

He looks at me questioningly.

"What?"

"I want the truth." He frowns. "Did you sleep with her?"

Confused, I ask, "Who?" As it dawns on me, it pisses me off at the same time. "The fed? I haven't touched her." I lift my hands. "And I'm offended you'd ask."

"So what your father said earlier wasn't true?"

"Not even close," I say, shaking my head. "It's a long story that I'd rather not get into. Trust me."

He nods. "You'll understand when you have a daughter."

I clear my throat. "I get it. Speaking of, I don't like the idea of you being here, and Reese having one less person watching out for her."

"I've got people informed. She's going to be fine. Let's focus on putting your father behind bars and getting you home. Is that your Mustang?" he asks, glancing at the shot up car parked behind him.

"Yeah, it's a rental."

He looks around. "I'll follow you home."

'm on my third beer. Andrew and I are lounging on the couch watching baseball. After I'd showed him where I lived, he parked down the street and walked here. We didn't want to look suspicious, in case someone spotted his car.

Chance has followed him into the kitchen, the bathroom, and everywhere between. Andrew pats him on the head. "That's a good boy," he tells him. Chance closes his eyes, then lies on his feet.

"What are you, the dog whisperer?"

He chuckles. "I don't know what it is, to be honest." He watches him fall asleep. "Must have been lonely here without him. I was worried about that."

Getting up to grab another beer, I reply, "Yeah it sucked, but I managed. Hey, you want something?"

He shows me his glass. "Water's good. Thanks." He quit drinking years ago. I envy him for that.

Sitting back on the couch, I ask him, "Did you see Reese before you left?"

"I did," he says, clasping his hands together. "Told her I was going away for a while, leading her to believe I was having a mid-life crisis." He purses his lips.

"She handle it okay?" I take a sip of my beer.

"Better than I expected. We had a breakthrough actually. She invited me to see her place." He grips my shoulder. "That was a selfless act of kindness what you did — giving her that home."

My mouth tips up at the corners. "I wanted her to have it the moment I walked into that old, worn-down apartment," I say, finishing my beer. I crush the can in my hand then climb off the couch and go grab another.

When I open the can, I pause. Andrew's eyes are on me. "What?"

"How often are you drinking?"

I cock a brow. "You're not about to lecture me, are you?"

"Not a lecture." Moving his feet out from under Chance, he lifts them onto the table. "They were falling asleep," he explains. "Anyway, if I remember correctly, you had told me you quit."

"I did," I tell him, taking a sip. "This is a relapse. Consider it temporary." I take a couple more, before setting it down.

"What is that? Your fifth?"

"Fourth. Are you really counting?" I let out a sardonic laugh. "If you think I can live this way sober, then you're crazy."

"Yeah, you're probably right," he says, blowing out a breath. "As long as you're smart enough to know the alcohol doesn't take your problems away. It only masks them."

"You're preaching to the choir, Andrew. So where are you staying anyway?"

"A historic hotel not all that far from here, and I'm hoping to be checked out within a day or two." He scratches his chin, then gets up and helps himself to another glass of water. Chance hops up and follows behind him—like he wasn't just sleeping a second ago.

He walks back into the living room. "I should go," he says, gulping down the remnants in his glass. "You never know when you could have a visitor." He's right. "Call me if anything comes up," he adds, setting the glass on the counter.

"Hey, you didn't answer my question earlier."

He raises his brows. "What was that?"

"The mess I'm in … is it the reason you grew out the beard? You knew you'd have to come here all along?"

His eyes light up, and he plays with his beard, tugging at his chin. "That's a mystery you may never solve."

"Aw, c'mon, tell me." I laugh. "Don't leave me hanging."

But he opens the door and walks out.

# 17

## Reese

When Sean said he was taking me out, this was *not* what I'd expected, but I swear I'm not complaining. I've only heard about it from friends. I'm kind of excited to see it in action. "Karaoke night, huh?" I ask, finding us our seats in the dimly lit bar that isn't quite filled up yet.

He flashes his award-winning smile, deciding on one of the booths that are lined up along the wall, facing the stage. "I think we'll fit in just fine, considering we're casual. You going to get up there and sing?" He raises an eyebrow.

"Not on your life!" I tell him. We just finished *Anchorman 2* less than ten minutes ago, then he suggested this hole-in-the-wall bar. It's been a long time since I've laughed as hard as I did during the movie. It felt good.

"We'll see about that once we get some drinks in you. Everything's on me." I consider this for a moment and decide not to argue. I still haven't told him about Luke. Maybe it'll be easier for him to accept after he has some alcohol in his system. He doesn't strike me as the angry-drinker type.

A scantily dressed cocktail waitress greets us at our table. I admire her raven black hair, cut in a sophisticated bob. Her eyes roam over Sean's body like he's something to eat. "I'll have a tall Sam Adams, please," he says, dropping his gaze to his phone. She appraises him a little longer, before her eyes move over to me.

I decide a drink might benefit the both of us and order one for myself. "I'll have a Captain and coke," I tell her. "Actually, can you make that diet, please?" I give her the friendliest smile I can muster. She gives me a look that says I'm the scum at the bottom of her shoe, then quickly struts to the bar.

"She's a real treat," I say, still watching her.

"Who?" Sean asks, still distracted with his phone.

"Is everything okay? Do you need to make a call or something?"

He shakes his head, then clears his throat. "Sorry about that. It was a text from a client of mine. You were saying?"

"Oh, it's no big deal. I just don't think our waitress likes me," I murmur back.

His brows pinch together. "Do you want to go somewhere else?"

"Of course not. I think she's got the hots for you, and it bothered her you didn't notice." I wiggle my eyebrows up and down, giving a subtle hint.

"Really?" he grins. "Is she hot?"

"Besides the fact that she dresses a little trashy and doesn't have much of a personality, yeah I'd say so."

He nods. "I'll have to check her out when she brings back our drinks." He taps on the table.

*Good, he's interested.* "You should ask for her number," I suggest.

He looks at me funny. "Bet she doesn't hold a candle to you."

"She's really cute," I reply, tugging down my shorts that are riding up too high.

A moment later, our waitress is back. "Rum and coke," she says, slamming the drink down in front of me, so hard that some of it spills over the side. "And here's your tall Sam Adams, baby," she purrs, her hand lingering on the mug longer than normal.

Sean answers with a cocky grin, his eyes on me. "Thanks. That'll be all for now," he tells her, raising his mug.

"You change your mind, honey, I'm right around the corner," she replies before slowly walking away, adding an extra sway to her hips.

"Wow, she's really trying to send you a message, Sean."

"You jealous?" His eyes sparkle at me.

"Jealous? No. But for all she knows I could be your girlfriend. Talk about a lack of respect for other women." I sip on my drink, which *surprisingly* isn't diet.

He gulps down his entire beer in one shot, wiping his mouth with the back of his hand. "Man, I needed that." He exhales. "By the way, you're cute when you're jealous."

I roll my eyes. "I'm *not* jealous. Did you hear what I just said?"

He chuckles. "Yeah, I heard you. I hadn't noticed the waitress. I was too busy paying attention to you."

"What?" *Uh oh.* I know that look. There's no way out of this talk. I look around and grab my glass, taking a big gulp. It hurts going down. I do one of those choke-coughs, trying to look as natural as I can, but my eyes are watering.

"I'll go get us more drinks," he says, snapping me out of my thoughts. "I think our girl's busy. Captain and diet, right?" he asks, pointing to my glass.

"Yes, thank you." I clear my throat. "Keep an eye on her this time. The last one was regular."

Broadening his shoulders, he says, "All right. Come get me if anyone bothers you." With his nearly six-foot frame, and a body that's packed in muscle, I doubt it's something he needs to worry about.

"I think I'll be okay." I smile before he walks away. I turn my attention back to the stage. The DJ lays out several books of music, and people wait in line to pick their song.

"You sure you don't want to sing?" Sean asks, setting down our drinks before sliding in the seat across from me.

Lady Gaga plays in the background. "Trust me. You don't want to hear me sing, but *you* go right ahead. I'll even record it," I tell him, flashing my phone.

"Couple more of these and I might."

I'm pretty sure he's kidding, but I go ahead and ask, "Do you sing?"

His mouth curves into a grin. "Not typically, but there's a chance I'll make an exception."

Florescent lights flicker around us, and a group of girls head over to the stage. An older man straggles behind them, wearing clothes that look to be from the seventies. He's fist pumping with a smile on his face. They tighten their circle and try to ignore him, but he's not giving up so easily.

"Check him out," Sean says with a cackle.

"I know. They're all avoiding him like the plague, but he just keeps on pumping those fists." I laugh.

"You women are harsh."

I take a sip of my drink. "Sometimes," I say, then ask, "So why'd you choose here of all places?"

He folds his arms, leaning back, then flashes his perfect grin. "Is that a good thing or bad?"

"A good thing," I tell him right away, hoping the question didn't offend him. "More relaxed. I pictured something else for some reason—with you being a *lawyer and all*," I joke.

"You mean more extravagant?" he cocks a brow, tilting his head.

"Yeah. Is that bad? Not that I expected anything fancy. I just didn't realize you came to places like this. It's refreshing actually. I'm happy you brought me here. It's fun," I reassure him.

Taking a drink, he says, "I get what you're saying. Let's see, how do I word this?" His brows pinch together. "You're different from most girls I know." He shrugs. "Down to Earth. This type of environment is comfortable for you." His eyes drift to the stage. "Look."

I follow his gaze, spotting woman holding a microphone in her hand. A song by Beyonce plays over the speakers. When the microphone meets her lips, she belts out the words with confidence.

"Dear Lord that's awful!" he says.

I flick my eyes back to Sean. His fingers are in his ears, and his brown eyes twinkle. "Get your fingers out of your ears." I swat him. I couldn't imagine if I was in her place and saw someone doing that. The process of getting up there alone is frightening enough.

"What?" He laughs, taking them out. "It's pure torture!"

"You wanted to come here, so you better be nice." I finish my drink and raise my brows at him, showing I mean business.

"Fine." He spots my empty glass. "You want another?"

I hold out a hand. "No thanks. But I'd really love some water," I say, already feeling a little tipsy.

The waitress appears at our table just in time. "You ready for another one?" she asks, only looking at Sean.

This time he actually glances at her. "Sure, and don't forget the lovely lady over here. She would like some water," he says, gesturing toward me.

She turns and makes her way around the bar, never once acknowledging me.

A man takes over the microphone, trying to channel Ed Sheeran. Sadly, he isn't any better than the last. Sean is on his best behavior, keeping his hands on the table, which only makes it harder to hold back my laugh.

"Okay, I'll admit it. Maybe they need a little practice, but who are we to judge them?"

He sips on his beer. "You're right. We shouldn't," he says, grinning. "Tell me you're having a good time."

"I'm having a *very* good time," I tell him, smiling back.

"Thank you."

"For what?" I ask, confused.

"For saying yes," he murmurs, looking at me the same way he had done earlier. "You deserve some fun every now and then." Leaning in close, he gently brushes his thumb over my cheek.

I swallow. "Thank you for not giving up on me," I say uncomfortably.

"Go out with me again."

My stomach sinks, knowing I'm about to hurt him. "Sean, I can't."

"I won't take no for an answer."

"There's something I need to tell you."

"Let me take you out. We'll go somewhere *extravagant* next time."

"No, it doesn't have to do with that. Just let me explain."

"It doesn't matter. You're coming with me."

My eyes widen. "Sean!" I say louder, getting his full attention. "Will you be quiet and listen?" I look around, wishing I didn't have to talk so loud to be heard over the music.

He nods, finally encouraging me to talk.

I drop my gaze to the table, not wanting to see the hurt in his eyes. "Luke and I, we … sort of patched things up," I mutter, chewing on my lip. "I wasn't sure how to tell you. You've always been …" I trail off, searching for the right words.

"Why'd he leave you? What was his excuse?" he asks, sounding pissed.

"Huh?" My eyes flick up to his. I heard him, but I don't know how to answer without making the situation worse than it already is.

"What was his excuse?" he asks again.

"I wish I could help you understand," I say, holding back a rush of tears. He's helped me though several months of pain and rejection, and this is what I give him back.

"Are you crying?" He sighs.

"Yes, I just don't want to lose you as a friend. You mean too much to me. I don't like that I'm hurting you." I sniffle, tearing apart the napkin that was put there for my drink.

"Stop worrying about me, Reese. I'll be fine. We'll always be friends. Worry about yourself right now." His jaw clenches. "Whether you believe it or not, the guy is playing you. How can you not see that?" His brows bunch together, and he grabs my hand, running his thumb over the back. "Did he give you an explanation?"

"Yes, he did, but I don't want to talk about that right now. Please don't give me a hard time about this," I beg. "I need your support."

"I know, and I'm trying, but don't forget who wiped away your tears the last few months, while that jerk off was out doing whatever."

Meeting his eyes, I say, "You have every reason to be upset."

Leaning in closer, he replies, "I'm not going anywhere. When you need me, I'll be here."

I didn't miss the *when* in his statement, but I know he's just watching out for me. "Thank you. That really means a lot.

"Don't mention it," he replies, but I can tell he's still upset.

We continue to chat through another hour of karaoke before Sean eventually calls us a cab, refusing to let me pay for anything. Luckily, our conversation steered away from the subject of my relationship with Luke, and the rest of the night we had a really good time. It's always that way with him.

# 18
## Luke

"Luke, get up."

Opening my eyes, I see Warren standing over me. I'd fallen asleep on my couch with the gun in my hand. I wasn't sure if those douchebags would come back and try to finish the job. After Andrew left, I drank the rest of the twelve-pack and passed out in my underwear. Lowering my weapon, I search the room for Chance. "How the hell did you get in here?"

He swings his thumb over his shoulder. "Door was unlocked. Get some clothes on. We need to go," he says, tipping his head toward the hall.

Feeling like I'd been hit by a truck, I rest my elbows on my knees, squinting my eyes shut. "Where the hell is my dog?"

"Haven't seen him," he replies, eyes roaming the interior of the house. Empty beer cans lie across the table.

As I stand, a wave of nausea hits me, and I sit back down, pressing my fingers to my temples. "Shit. I feel sick. Where are we going?"

"To meet the guys," he answers, lifting his chin. "They're waiting for us."

"What time is it?" I flinch, accidently rubbing the wound on my head.

"Time to put your pants on. Question me in the car."

"Where the hell's my dog?" I ask him again, ready to pummel somebody.

"I already told you! How the hell would I know? Will you get off the couch already?"

"Stop hovering over me like a mother hen. I'll get up when I'm ready to get up," I snap. My head is fucking killing me.

"How much did you drink?"

"Too much," I answer, standing up and making my way into the kitchen, still searching for Chance. When I spot him on the patio, I let him in, and he sniffs Warren out.

Warren crouches down, petting him with both hands. "You remember me. Don't-cha boy?"

Chance responds with a few sloppy licks to the face. Warren laughs and wipes the slobber away, then stares at me while I stare at him. *For the love of God,* would you put on some clothes?" Standing up, he leans against the counter.

Grabbing a bottle of ibuprofen out of the medicine cabinet, I pop some into my mouth and swallow. "Never took you for a dog person," I tell him.

He shrugs. "Never had a problem with them."

"Didn't seem that way in the desert." He hadn't been thrilled about bringing Chance in the car after we found him.

"Maybe he's growing on me."

"Uh huh." Leaving him with my dog, I tread toward my room to throw on some clothes. Ten minutes later we're driving down the highway in a Yukon I've never seen him drive before. I assume it's probably stolen.

"Why'd you pick me up?" I ask. Not that I would have driven—or answered any calls. Luckily, my headache is easing up a little.

"Glenn gave me orders," he replies.

I raise my brows. "To come to my house without a heads-up? Where's Marcus?" They always ride together.

"He's with Glenn," he says, looking straight ahead. "Something happened tonight. Glenn wants to discuss it."

*Of course he does.* "Discuss it?" I ask, glancing at the clock. "It couldn't wait 'til the sun came up? Does the man ever sleep?" I rake a hand through my hair.

"I doubt it," Warren replies. "If he does, he keeps his eyes open."

"What is it we're discussing exactly?" I ask, answering my own question as soon as the words leave my mouth. *Valdez.*

"We're about to find out," he says, glancing at me sideways before gazing back at the road. "Say your prayers," he adds, shaking his head. "Shit's about to go down tonight. That's all I'm sayin'."

I stare out the window. "That's comforting." We're driving in unfamiliar territory. Everything looks secluded.

"You sobered up a little?" Warren asks, cocking a brow.

"Actually, I am."

"Good. You're gonna need your head for this."

My gaze snaps to his. "There something you wanna tell me?" Taking an exit off of the highway, we head south. I roll down the window for fresh air, nervous about what I'm walking into.

"I already did," he says, turning off the road, heading into the desert. He checks his GPS, though I doubt anything with a heartbeat could live out here.

"Could you elaborate a bit?"

He makes a right turn. "Afraid I can't." Driving straight ahead, we climb over some rocky hills, before a worn-down shack comes into view. A few figures stand behind it.

Turning off the headlights, he kills the engine. "Like I said, say your prayers." He opens the door and gets out. I do the same, walking through the desert in the dark. The sound of the gravel crunching beneath my feet is heightened by our surroundings. We're in the middle of nowhere, and my eyes are still trying to adjust.

A flashlight shines in our direction, allowing us to see our way around the shed. I spot four other figures gathered together, recognizing my father in the middle, his taller frame standing out.

"Great place you found here. You going to tell me what's going on?" All the men are visibly armed, each one with their eyes on me. Two of them I've never met before—one of them tall, the other short. The only light comes from the flashlight in Marcus's hand, and it's aimed at the ground.

"Son." My father grins, stepping toward me. "Always the last to arrive, though I'm glad you were able to make it. I hope this wasn't too much of an inconvenience for you," he says, meaning the opposite.

"Maybe next time I could have a little more notice."

"I'll take note of that," he says, turning around with his hands clasped behind his back. "A close friend of mine was arrested tonight." He pauses. "He will most likely spend the rest of his life in prison."

My eyes flick to the rest of the men. There isn't an ounce of surprise on their faces, which leads me to believe this speech is solely meant for me. So why the hell are we in the middle of nowhere at this time of night?

I watch as he paces back and forth with pursed lips. "This close friend of yours … have I met him?"

"The two of you met the other day," he replies. "Sergio Valdez." His brown eyes peer into mine.

Trying to look disappointed, I say, "I'm sorry, but I'm curious. Why tell us here?" I glance around in the darkness.

"I'm getting to that," he replies, stepping toward me. "Unfortunately, Valdez had a leak in his circle." He sighs. "All these years he'd been extremely careful ..." He looks at me appraisingly. "But one small mistake cost him everything." Silence. "We can't afford to make mistakes." His eyes flick over his shoulder. "Men."

The two men I don't recognize leave their positions and enter the shed. Marcus shines the flashlight on the haggard building. The fingers of my right hand twitch over my gun. "What's going on?"

A deviant grin slides across my father's face. "Once I found out about Valdez's arrest, I made a few calls." He lifts his chin. "Years ago, I'd learned a lesson the hard way. It's important to have connections wherever you may need them, especially in the type of businesses I run. You understand?"

I nod.

"Some may call them informants, others may call them leaks. There are several names you could call them ..." Pausing, he cocks a brow. "Isn't that right, Drew?"

*No.* Turning at the waist, I see the two men dragging a person out of the shed. Marcus shines the flashlight on his face, and my pulse spikes. It's Andrew. He's barely conscious and covered in blood. My hands clench into fists.

"Hold him up," my father tells them. Andrew's too weak to stand on his own. Blood drips from his face, as his head hangs in defeat. Those assholes have been torturing him. Warren watches my reaction after the men grab Andrew from underneath his shoulders and lift him up. Andrew flinches, moaning in pain. He hasn't made eye contact with me, but he knows where I am.

My father steps toward him, bending down so they're at eye level. "I said, isn't that right, Drew?" he taunts.

A small chuckle escapes from Andrew's throat, then he spits in my father's face. Marcus points the light at the saliva sliding down Glenn's cheek. He wipes it away with fury in his gaze, smacking Andrew with the back of his hand. Then one by one the men take their turns kicking him — the shorter one kicking him in the head. Marcus snickers behind me. I can't watch this anymore.

"Enough!" my father says sharply at the moment I nearly snap. Andrew is writhing on the ground, groaning in pain. "We came here for a reason," he states, eyes flicking to me. "Luke, consider this a lesson."

"In what? Torture?" I hiss. "Look at the man," I motion toward his broken body.

Narrowing his gaze on me, he says, "Do not interrupt me."

I'm not sure how much longer I can hold back my rage.

"It has been brought to my attention that our new partner over here," he snarls, "is working for the DEA."

Furrowing my brows, I ask, "Who told you that? How can you be sure?"

"I have my sources, son, and I can assure you, they're all credible. I won't mention any names."

"That's disappointing." I pause, thinking. "What do you say we leave him to rot — head home and grab some shuteye?"

"You know that isn't an option."

I gaze at all the men. "The DEA could be watching us. Are you willing to take that risk?"

They snicker along with my father.

"You don't think we've checked into that?" His eyes are filled with amusement. "Clearly you've underestimated me, son. He needs to be terminated," he says, flicking his gaze to Andrew. He places his hands on my shoulders. "Finish the job. Before daylight to be most efficient."

"If we leave him, he'll be dead by morning. He's nearly dead already," I point.

"You're forgetting about the evidence."

"We'll come back in the morning—burn the body."

He gets in my face. "Execute him, Luke, or I'll do it myself, and you can spend the rest of your life killing the women and children who get in our way. Is that what you'd prefer?"

"Of course not!" I snap.

"That's what I thought," he says, taking a few steps back. "Now hurry up. We've wasted enough time."

I swallow, slowly lifting my gun to aim at Andrew. The rest of the men are clutching their AKs in their hands, as they watch with stoic faces.

"Shoot him!" Glenn hisses, losing his patience.

Marcus stands behind me, breathing down the back of my neck.

My jaw clenches. "What the hell, man!" Headbutting him, I jab him in the gut with an elbow. He bowls over, and I snatch his AK, slamming it into his face.

Glenn shouts behind me as Marcus goes down. "We don't have time for this shit! Fuck it!" I hear a click.

Spinning around, I find my father pointing a gun at Andrew, ready to shoot. I aim, then pull the trigger right as his gun goes off. Glenn's head disintegrates. Diving to the ground, I crawl closer to Andrew, all while getting shot at.

"Andrew!" I lie beside him, losing feeling in one of my legs. A sharp pain hits my shoulder. I flinch, as I try to lift my gun.

"Glenn's gone now," I say, unsure if he can hear me. "She's going to be okay." It's getting harder to breathe. "Don't die on me, buddy." I'm crying silent tears before the world fades away, and I'm sucked into the darkness.

# 19

## Reese

By the time we arrive at the hospital, I'm confused and distraught. Until this moment I hadn't realized how much I want and need my father in my life. Now it looks like I'm going to lose him again. This time, though, it'll be for forever. Our relationship has been a complicated one, but he promised that he'd changed, and we were on the mend.

We've spent more time with each other these last few months than in my entire life. He's become more than a father; he's a friend. In the beginning, I put up a wall because I was scared — protecting myself from his rejection — but now I realize that I became the rejecter. I wipe the wetness from my face while we scurry over to the nurse's station in the ICU.

My cell buzzes in my pocket, my hands trembling when I pull it out and see Pam's number flash across the screen. Relief washes over me, but I'll call her back later. For a moment I was terrified the call was from the hospital, informing me that my father had passed away, and we were too late.

I pace the room, worrying my lip between my teeth, trying to understand what might have put him in this situation. *What happened to you, Dad? They said you were shot? Who would do this?*

*Was it an accident? Is there something you've been keeping from me?* I cringe at the thought that it might *not* have been an accident.

My phone buzzes again, and I ignore it. Pam will have to wait. If my dad can hold on a little longer, I'll try and get the truth from him and tell him all the things I've been too prideful to say — that I love him, I forgive him, and that everybody makes mistakes. I want to tell him I'm sorry. I'm sorry for being such a stubborn brat, and I truly believe he's changed for the better. I want to thank him for finally being the father I need, and tell him I don't hold it against him anymore for when he wasn't. I've forgiven him. I forgave him a long time ago. There's so much I still need to say. It can't be time for him to go yet.

"Okay Reese," Gia says, grabbing my shoulders. "Look at me. 301. That's his room number." She forces me to make eye contact. "The nurse says only one can go in at a time, and only family. Are you going to be okay in there by yourself?" Her eyes are warm, and she sighs. "I wish I could go with you."

"I'll be fine," I murmur, licking my now dry lips, needing some water. My nerves are dehydrating me.

"You ready to go in?"

"As ready as I can be." The nausea is swirling in my stomach, and I'm not sure I'll be able to handle the sight of him lying alone in a hospital bed, fighting for his life.

The only time I've seen him vulnerable was the night he'd come to my work, begging me to give him another chance. And I told him I didn't want to see him anymore. What kind of daughter does that?

More tears spill down my cheeks, and I turn to Gia. "Can you do me a favor?" I ask, wiping my face.

"Anything."

"Can you have Logan call Pam ... let her know what's going

on?"

"Already on it." She nods. "He took the call outside. The reception here sucks."

"Thank you. I don't think I'll be able to talk." I'm stalling, afraid of what I'm going to find. "I'm scared."

Hugging me again before she shoos me forward, she says, "Go see your dad."

I hand her my phone. "If my mom calls, tell her everything," I say over my shoulder, walking down the narrow hall. "I don't want him to overhear me talking about him. Tell her I'll call as soon as I can." God, I pray he's conscious. Just the thought of it makes me walk faster.

"Will do! Good luck!" she yells back. "I love you. Take all the time you need," she adds.

Swallowing the lump that's been lodged in my throat, I make my way around the corner, then walk all the way down to the end to find room 301.

The moment I spot my father's lifeless body I freeze, hoping I've made some kind of mistake. He looks like a stranger, bloodied and broken, hooked up to every kind of medical machine imaginable. His chest rises and falls with the assistance of a plastic tube shoved down his throat. Of all the scenarios I've played out in my head, nothing could have prepared me for this.

An uncontrollable sob escapes me, and I cover my mouth, trying to muffle the sound, which only makes me cry harder. They told me he'd been shot, and that he was alive, but his condition was deteriorating. They never mentioned *life support*. I guess I was being optimistic. After hearing *alive* I stopped paying attention.

My eyes fall to one of his hands, and I hesitate before placing my own inside of it.

"Daddy?" I squeeze, hoping that for some miraculous reason, the sound of my voice will snap him out of this unconscious state. Maybe it's wishful thinking, but I at least need to try. I get nothing, so I wait a little longer, moving my gaze to his swollen face. The top of his head is all wrapped up in gauze. I don't even know how many times he was shot, or where. From the looks of it, I'd say he was shot in the head.

I pull down the sheet a little, finding multiple bandages on his chest, which I assume are more gunshot wounds. This definitely wasn't an accident. Somebody wanted him dead. I cover my mouth, a little scared and in shock.

"What happened to you, Dad?" I cry. "Who did this?" My father never mentioned enemies. At the same time, he isn't the type who likes to be the subject of conversation, always keeping the focus on me. Now I'm wondering if he had good reason.

A nurse walks in to check on his vitals. "Hello. Don't mind me, I'll be quick," she says, taking her time, reading over the monitor, before her eyes flick down to my father. I can see her concern, but she masks it when she turns and gives me a warm smile. "All done. I'll leave you two alone now." And just like that, she disappears, not giving me a chance to ask her any questions.

Spotting the chair behind me, I move it close to the bed, so I can still hold his hand while I talk to him. But I'm so emotionally exhausted, I don't have the strength to stand anymore. Watching the way his chest fills with air and then releases is disturbing. It looks unnatural. It *is* unnatural. Is he unable to breathe without it? Is it really just these machines that are keeping him alive?

"Dad ..." My voice cracks as I look at his face. "I'm here. You're not alone anymore. Okay? C-can you hear me?" I say, asking through the tears. I want him to hear everything, but it's hard to hold back a sob with each word, and my throat is closing up. Linking my fingers with his, I'm startled by how lifeless and cold they feel. "I love you, Daddy. Can you hear me?" I lean over to kiss him on the cheek. "I said I love you. I love you *so* much," I choke. "And I'm … I'm sorry for not saying it to you earlier. I was scared—I was scared you'd leave again, so I tried to fight it. It didn't matter though because you squeezed your way back into my heart anyway, and I enjoyed every minute of it."

My eyes flick up to the heart monitor that spiked for a few seconds, before returning to its normal pace. "I'm sorry for the way I treated you that day at the restaurant. I feel horrible about it, and I don't think … I don't think I ever apologized. I was being immature, trying to hurt you. If I could, I would take it all back. You know I forgive you for everything, don't you?" More sobbing ensues before I can pull it together enough to speak again. "I hope you can forgive me, too."

Grabbing a tissue off of the nearby end table, I wipe what looks like a tear coming from the corner of his eye. "Do you hear me, Daddy?" Squeezing his hand, I'm both excited and terrified at the sight. "Are you in pain?" Oh God, I hope he's not in pain and unable to tell anybody about it.

"It means so much to me that you looked for me after all these years … that you wrote me all of those letters. You never gave up on me." I rub my thumb over the back of his hand, holding it against my face. "I'm not giving up on you either."

A slight movement in his fingers captures my attention, and then he's squeezing me back. Suddenly, he starts convulsing on top of the bed. My eyes widen, and I jump out of the chair, running down the hall in a panic. "Help!" I scream. "I need a nurse! "Somebody help! Please, I don't know what's happening!"

The nurse I saw earlier, along with three others, rush past me, making their way into his room, before they slam the door in my face. I take a couple steps back, until I hit the wall and slide down. Resting my forehead on my knees, feeling helpless, I say a silent prayer.

# 20

## Reese

It didn't take long before the nursing staff began trailing out of his room, acting as if he wasn't just seizing on his bed. It was both comforting and confusing. As soon as I was allowed, I resumed my post at his bedside.

"You must be Reese," the nurse I'd seen an hour earlier says, holding out her hand as she enters the room. A warm smile stretches across her face. "My name is Michelle. I'm the nurse on duty for the night." Nudging her head toward my dad, she says, "Rumor has it this man is your father."

"That would be a fact," I answer.

"I can see the resemblance," she replies, glancing back and forth between us. She's probably in her thirties, with long brown hair and big hazel eyes—she's pretty.

Turning my attention back to my dad, I pick up his hand again. "Everybody says that."

She grins. "How's he been doing since the episode? Any luck getting a response?" There's sadness in her expression, like she already knows the answer. *She did just check his vitals after all.*

"No," I murmur, clearing my dry throat. "I haven't been able to get anything from him."

They gave my father some anti-seizure medication to stop the convulsing. I guess the shaking is pretty common for a person in his state—at least that's what they told me. For a brief moment I felt relief. But then another nurse mentioned his kidneys were no longer functioning, and it wouldn't take long before the rest of his organs followed suit. *In other words, she told me he's dying.* And there went any small hope I'd held on to.

"I'm not the type to give up without a fight, though," I say, glancing at him. "Neither is he."

"That's the spirit," she replies with a hand on her hip. "I doubt he'd give up on *you* if *you* were in his position."

*I wish I were.*

"You're right. He wouldn't." There's nothing worse than a pessimistic doctor or nurse. I'm thankful she isn't one of them. "Is there anything I can do to help him?"

"You're doing it," she says, eyeing our connected hands. "Talk to him, hold his hand, tell him you love him, maybe read him his favorite book." She's about to say something else then pauses, before opening her mouth again to speak. "I hope this doesn't upset you," she says, slowly stepping toward me with concern in her face.

A sick feeling starts to settle in my gut.

"I overheard the things you said to your father earlier."

Relieved, I close my eyes. "Believe me, that's the least of my worries," I say, my palm over my chest. "For a moment, I thought you were about to tell me somebody died." I glance back at him.

"He may not look it, but he knows you're here. What you said earlier was perfect."

My eyes fill with tears. "Do you think he heard me?" Her words mean more than she'll ever know.

Her brows shoot up. "Oh, most definitely," she replies. "Don't let anybody tell you differently." Brushing her fingers over his head, she says, "They say that hearing is the last to go. Keep talking to him. He's knows you're here with him."

"Thank you." I really want to believe her.

"That's why I'm here." As she fixes my father's bedding, she asks him if he's comfortable. He doesn't respond, of course, but it's a nice gesture.

She's already been pretty helpful, so I'm hoping she'll answer some of my other questions. "Michelle."

She lifts her chin to acknowledge me.

"Do you know what happened to him?"

By her hesitant expression, she was clearly hoping I wouldn't ask.

Placing her hands in her pockets, she nervously glances at the door. "What have you heard exactly?" She's speaking quietly enough so nobody else can hear.

"They told me he was shot. That's it. But I know it wasn't an accident. Look at him," I whisper, tipping my head.

"I know. Anybody could tell that with one glance."

"I haven't seen the rest of him, but I've seen the bandages on his chest." I say, covering my face with both hands. "Oh God, how long did he suffer before somebody brought him in?" Tears are spilling once again. "I saw him just a few days ago, and he said he was going out of town. He isn't supposed to be here!" I sob.

Pressing a finger to her lips, Michelle says, "Give me a quick second. Okay?" I nod and watch her walk through the doorway. Someone standing in the hall exchanges a few words with her, before she comes back in, closing the door completely.

"I can get in a lot of trouble for this," she says, making her way over. "If I tell you what I know, will you promise not to tell anybody?" She's biting her lip nervously. "I could lose my job."

"Yeah … yeah, of course," I whisper. I would never rat her out for helping me.

"There's been a cop standing right outside this door ever since your father arrived. As soon as you showed up, though, he left. I assume he maybe knew who you were."

I nod, wondering if he's a friend of my dad's—someone I possibly know. Remembering the card my father gave me the other day, I ask, "Do you know what his name is? Or what agency he works for?" I grab my wallet out of my purse and pull out the card.

"No, I don't have a name. They're very secretive around here."

"My father gave me this," I say, showing her the front of it. "He told me to call this man if I ran into trouble." The name on the card reads: *Thomas Sullivan*. "It didn't make sense to me at the time, but now I wonder if it's linked. Is there a phone I can use? I'm going to call him."

"You'll have to use the phone at the nurses' desk. The staff was told to remove his courtesy phone."

I tilt my head, confused. "That's fine. I'll use my cell phone. My friend has it in the waiting room. Why would you remove his phone?"

"Law enforcement has been in contact with our Chief of Staff. We were told it's for the safety of the patient. They also explained that only immediate family members are allowed to visit the patients."

"Wait a minute. Patients? As in more than one?"

Paranoid, she glances toward the window. "Your father was flown here at 4:28 AM with multiple gunshot wounds … one of them to the head," she says, sneaking a sideways glance at him. "They took him straight into surgery. The other …" she adds, before pausing with pursed lips.

"The other?" My eyes widen, and I urge her to keep going. Afraid she isn't going to tell me, I beg, "Please. I'm not going to say anything."

"Okay, okay. He wasn't alone. There. I said it." She closes her eyes, sighing.

Taking a seat in the chair behind me, I ask, "Someone else was injured with him?"

She nods. "There were several. All of them with gunshot wounds. Most of them were dead when they arrived," Michelle says, looking from side to side. "The buzz around here is it was some kind of drug bust, but that's a rumor. With all the cops roaming the place, people start talking."

I hadn't noticed any cops, but then again, I wasn't looking. "So where are they now?"

"Oh, they're *everywhere*; not in uniform, though. They're undercover. It's easy to tell with some of them, by the way they carry themselves."

"Ah, now I get it." I turn toward my father. "You didn't tell me what you were really planning to do, because you knew I'd try to talk you out of it," I say, staring at his face. "I guess that answers my questions about the beard." Leaning down, I press a kiss against his forehead. "Look what they did to you. Don't let them win, okay?" My gaze flicks back toward Michelle.

"You said there were other survivors who came in with him?"

Clearing her throat, she says, "Yes, just one other."

"Do you know if he's a cop?"

"No. I wouldn't have that information. I'm sorry."

"So it's possible that the person who did this," I say, pointing at my dad, "might be on this very floor?" That concerns me more than anything.

"Shh!" She glances toward the door. "All I'm saying is that he isn't the only survivor. I don't know anything about the condition of the person or people who did this to him. What I *do* know is, it's best if you leave the investigating to law enforcement, and stay out of this. Don't go snooping around. It could be dangerous. You seem like the kind of woman who won't stop until she gets her answers." Narrowing her eyes, she asks, "Am I right?"

"Maybe, but what's wrong with that?" I've got to call that Thomas guy.

"I just told you what's wrong with it," she points. "Does your father work in law enforcement?"

"Yes and no. It's a long story, and I don't want to ramble. He does some work under the table," I reply.

"Then let them take care of this. I'm not going to say any more. I've already said too much as it is."

I smile, reaching for her hand. "Thank you for all your help. And don't worry, my lips are sealed."

# 21

## Reese

It's been over twenty-four hours since my father's condition took a turn for the worse. After collecting my phone from Gia, I sent her and Logan home, not expecting her to wait all this time. She's been texting me every hour since. I told her to take a long nap, and stop feeling guilty for leaving. None of us had any sleep last night.

I left a voicemail for Thomas Sullivan then attempted to reach my mom again with no luck. I ended up falling asleep on a cot next to my dad, mentally drained and emotionally exhausted. He had another seizure-like episode, which resulted in him receiving more medication. Just like before, it freaked me out. Now I watch him lie here all doped up on several medications. It's not like I can tell the difference. In a way, it seems like I've lost him already.

Michelle told me last night that I would see the neurologist today. We're supposed to go over the results of my father's brain scan. He's looking less and less like himself, as time progresses, and I'm nervous with what the results will tell me. I'm losing my optimism at this point, but the last thing I want to do is discourage him from fighting. I just don't know if he's here anymore.

"Hello," comes the voice of a male behind me. Turning

around I see who I assume is the neurologist, as well as another man dressed in regular clothes. Both of them are older with gray hair, though the man in regular clothes is nearly bald. The other one holds out his hand. "I'm Dr. Belding. You must be?" he asks, raising his brows.

"Reese." I give a small grin, tipping my head toward my father. "I'm his daughter."

"Nice to meet you, Reese," he replies, gesturing to the man standing beside him. "This here is Pastor Sorenson."

The pastor smiles, his eyes kind. "I'm one of the chaplains here at the hospital."

My grin fades instantly. I can think of only one reason a neurologist would bring a chaplain with him, and it isn't a good one. "S-sorry," I stutter. "I don't mean to be rude. It's just—"

"I understand. Believe me, I get that look a lot. There's no need to apologize," he replies genuinely.

Knowing we should get to the point, I lift my chin and ask, "Is my dad brain dead?" I look each of them in the eye. Their expressions are solemn as they communicate to me silently. If they've come here to tell me he is, then I know the decision I'll be facing.

Silently, I wonder if they hate this part of their job—where they have to tell a person that their loved one is about to die … or already has.

The neurologist softly says, "He's gone, ma'am." "The scans show no blood flow to the brain. The reality of it is, your father will remain in a permanently vegetative state, as long as his heart keeps beating. To put it bluntly, these machines are keeping him alive."

I'm going to be sick. "What about the first brain scan? Yesterday, I saw a tear come out of his eye while I was talking to him." I'm grasping on to any hope I can find.

The doctor's brows pinch together. "The first brain scan was taken when he got here. That one *did* show some activity, but very little," he says, pinching with his fingers, indicating the smallest amount. "It's possible he was still with us when you talked to him."

"It's very possible," the chaplain says. "And I bet he heard you, too."

*I like this guy.*

"It's not uncommon for the first scan to show some activity and the second to come out flat," the neurologist adds. "Unfortunately, there's no blood flow going to his brain anymore."

I'm numb, slowly processing everything. I can't. I can't keep him on those machines. I know he wouldn't want it. We've talked about this before … *Oh my God, he's gone. My dad is gone.* Closing my eyes, the chaplain steps in, attempting to bring me words of comfort.

"Reese, do you know if your father was a believer?"

My eyes snap open to meet his compassionate gaze, and the floodgates swing open. I can no longer hold back. "Yes," I say, choking on a sob. "Yes, he was."

"That's good news. Understand that he is no longer in pain," he says sincerely. "Your father is in a better place now."

Covering my face as best I can, he squeezes my shoulder. "Are you here by yourself? We want to make sure you'll be okay."

"I … I am …" I hesitate. "It's just … this is a lot to take in, and they won't let anybody other than family in here. M-my m-mom is-n't call-ing m-me ba-ack." I can't even talk right now. It's all too much. I want Luke here with me, and I don't even have a way to get ahold of him. And now on top of everything else, I'm pissed at him for being gone when I need him.

"Do you have someone who can come get you?" the chaplain asks gently.

"Yeah I do," I say, licking my lips. "I just need to wrap my head around this for a second. I don't ... I don't think I can talk to anybody now." I'm not even looking at them anymore; I'm sort of in a daze. "Can you give me a little time?" I ask, wishing I could get ahold of my mom.

"We'll call for you if you'd like," he replies.

"Please." Digging through my purse, I forget what I'm looking for. *Oh yeah, my phone.* Once I find it, I scroll through the contacts and hand it over. "Her name is Gia."

He nods, before walking out of the room with my phone.

*My father's gone. My father's gone. My father's gone.* The phrase runs repeatedly through my head. His pale, lifeless body only confirms it.

"Your friend Gia's on her way up," the chaplain says, handing me my phone. When he asks if I'd let him pray with me, I agree, because I know my father would have wanted it.

Walking down the hall, in what seems like slow motion, I glance in every open room I pass—searching for a clue. Someone on this floor knows what happened to my father. I still haven't received a call back from that Thomas guy, but I plan to bug him until he talks to me. My father gave me his card, so it obviously means he trusts him.

Heels clanking against the tiled hospital floor captures my attention, and I wonder if my eyes are playing tricks on me. *No way.* I blink. *Why is she here?* Pausing, I stay back, watching as her blonde tresses bounce with each and every step. Of all the people,

Lauren Ryann scurries down the hall, her expression frazzled, as she messes with an arrangement of flowers. Thankfully, they hinder her view of me. If this weren't the worst day of my life, I'd check on her … make sure she's okay. I'm just glad she isn't crying. It'll lessen some of the guilt I'll feel for avoiding her.

Before her brother left, she'd moved up to Flagstaff with a close friend of hers. There's so much to catch up on, I wouldn't know what to say. She'll ask why I'm here, and then I'll have to explain. And I don't have the strength for that right now. I want to go home, lie in my bed, and listen to music.

Her eyes fall to the numbers on the doors. I think she's ready to turn the corner, but instead she stays on the same path. I panic, spotting the empty room to my right, then step inside and hide behind the doorway. It's childish, I know, but I don't care.

I peek around the wall and catch her walking into a room, shutting the door behind her. Blowing out a breath, I make my way toward the exit, trying to get as far away from this place as I possibly can. Thank God I don't have to drive today.

Michelle stops me at the nurses' station, meeting my eyes. Forcing a smile, I make a weak attempt at thanking her for all the encouragement. I wouldn't have opened up like I did, if it weren't for her advice. "Thank you," I cry. "For everything."

Her eyes tear up, then she pulls me into a hug. I wrap my arms around her, resting my head on her shoulder. We barely know each other, but it feels like we bonded last night. I can tell she's a good person, and I'm glad she was there.

"I am so sorry," she replies. The hug is exactly what I need. I close my eyes, enjoying the momentary comfort.

"Excuse me," we hear behind us.

I open my eyes, facing a stunning brunette who appears around my age. I think she may be lost. "Can I help you?"

Michelle asks, walking behind the help desk.

"Yes. A patient of yours was moved to a different room. Nobody told me where they put him."

Tapping on the keyboard, Michelle replies, "You look familiar. Is he in the ICU?"

"Yes. They admitted him two days ago."

"Gotcha. Tell me his name, hon. I'll see if I can find him." Glancing at me, she holds up a finger.

"Ryann," she answers, readjusting her purse. "His name is Luke Ryann."

My heart nearly drops into my stomach. *Wait. What?* Blinking twice—maybe three times—I'm flat out staring at this girl in shock.

"If you'd like, I'll mention you're here? Someone is in there with him right now. Unfortunately, he's only allowed one visitor at a time."

*Lauren.* I need to lie down. Lauren is visiting her brother. Her brother! Luke is hurt. What are the chances? He and my father at the same time? It can't be a coincidence. Can it?

"I assume you're family?"

"Yes. I've been here twice," the girl answers, irritated. I'm ready to ask her what's wrong with him.

"She's his wife," another nurse interrupts. "I've got this, Michelle. Looking for your husband?" A smile spreads across the nurse's face. "The air conditioner went out in the old room. So we moved Luke to 307. He's awake, and they're expecting you. Sorry 'bout that. Follow me. I'll take you to him."

# 22

## Luke

*Beep. Beep. Beep. Beep.* "Luke, can you hear me?" *Beep. Beep.* "Come on, big bro, wake up. I see you moving your fingers. Can you hear me?" I feel a tug at my hand. It sounds like I'm in a hospital room—beeping noises are all around me, and there are rails on my bed—but I'm having a hard time opening my eyes. Though it is good to hear my sister's voice. "Open them, Luke." Her face finally comes into view. A tear slides off her cheek.

"Hi." She smiles. "You're awake."

I grin back, feeling loopy, then attempt to say hello, but the word comes out raspy. More tears fall down Lauren's face. "Why are you crying?" Damn, it hurts to talk. "Is it that bad?" My eyes scan my body. I've got a shoulder and leg that are bandaged up pretty good.

"I thought I was going to lose you." She steps away for a second, coming back with a full vase of flowers in her hands. "I bought you these," she says, showing me the arrangement. "I was really hoping you'd get to see them before they died." She frowns, setting them down on the side table. "Looks like I got my wish."

I burst out in laughter, flinching from the pain. "You *would* buy me flowers," I say, coughing. "That's sweet of you, Lauren. Thanks. But you didn't need to buy me anything."

Concern shows on her face. "Do you need me to get the nurse—her name's Julie? Get you more pain meds? She's been real attentive to you, maybe has a little crush, but she's very sweet. She recently moved you from another room, because the AC had gone out."

I'm a little slow at taking all of that in. "That was nice of them," I reply.

"I can get her if you want?"

"In a minute," I say, trying to scoot up a little. It's hard to put pressure on my arm, and it hurts a lot more than I'm letting on. I don't want to be a pussy in front of my sister. It'll just make her worry about me. "I assume you have some questions."

"I do," she says, giving a single nod. There's a crease between her brows. "Although I can probably guess some of the answers." Her blue eyes meet mine. "I'm just glad you're okay, Luke," she adds, biting her quivering lip.

Lauren left Phoenix about six months ago after a bad break up. She and a friend wanted to see what it'd be like to live in a smaller town—so off they went to Flagstaff. Last time we spoke, I told her what I planned to do about Glenn. She didn't like the idea, but didn't try to stop me either. She knew my mind had been made up already.

"Come here." I stretch my arms out to give her a hug, but freeze halfway, the screaming pain in my shoulder reminding me of my injuries. "Ow."

She laughs and cries at the same time. "You look like a mummy."

I laugh with her and it hurts.

"Oh God. Sorry," she says. "Try not to laugh."

"How long was I out anyway?" I ask. "How long have I been here? I don't even know what day it is."

"Two days. They put you in a medically induced coma. Do you remember what happened?"

"I think I was shot."

She nods. "Once in the shoulder and twice in the leg."

Memories of the other night are flashing through my head. "What hospital are we at?" My eyes roam the white board on the wall across from me at the same time she answers.

"We're at Saint Joe's."

*Saint Joe's.* I'm in Phoenix. I search for a phone, then flinch again. I keep forgetting about my shoulder until it's too late. My drugs are wearing off, and my mind's becoming clearer. I've got to check on Andrew. Last time I saw him he was in bad shape.

"Careful," I hear from a voice not belonging to my sister. "It's time for your pain meds." A young nurse approaches me with sparkly eyes and a bright smile. At least she's a happy nurse.

"Let me guess. You're Julie?"

"That's me!" She grins. "*You're* handsome and awake," she says, winking. "How are we feeling?"

Flicking my gaze to Lauren, I catch her covering a smile with her hand. I'm not sure if Julie's being friendly, or if that was some sort of pick up line. "I've definitely felt better."

"I bet you have." She nods. "On a scale of one to ten, how bad is the pain?"

"I don't know. An eight or nine I guess."

"All right," she replies. "Don't worry. I'm going to take the pain away." She leans in close enough to make it uncomfortable, then says, "You have some gorgeous eyes — like pools of whiskey. I'd been betting on cobalt blue, back when you were asleep. These are even better."

"Thank you?" comes out more like a question, and I'm feeling a little violated. Lauren giggles in her chair.

"You're welcome." She stands and straightens her shoulders. "I'll go get your medicine. See this button right here ... press it if you need me," she says, pointing to a little red symbol on the remote that's connected to my bed. "I'll make sure they give your wife a ring. She'll be happy to hear you're awake and expecting her." At that, she darts out of the room, chart in hand.

My eyes move to Lauren. "Did she just say my wife?"

Biting her lip, she replies, "Yeah, I was going to ask you about that. Rachelle?" Her brows raise and I pause.

"Son of a—"

"I knew it wasn't true," she interrupts. "She told me if you wake up, to tell you the dog is okay," she adds, shrugging. "I figured I'd ask you about it later."

I rub the space between my brows. I'd forgotten about Chance. "Good, they got him," I sigh, glancing at her. "It's a long story. And you're right. It isn't true. I'm just too tired to explain right now." I'm reminded, once again, of Andrew. "Have you heard anything about Andrew?"

She looks at me, confused. "Who?"

"Reese's father—Andrew. Shit! I need the nurse!" Pressing the red button, I need to know, and now.

Lauren shoots out of her chair. "I'll go get her." She's panicking, as she rushes through the doorway. My expression probably scared her.

Moments later, they're hurrying back in the room. Julie places my meds on the tray with a small cup of water. "What is it, honey? What do you need?"

"The night I came here ... were there others with me?"

"Yes." She nods. "From what I understand."

I close my eyes and exhale a breath. I open them and ask, "How bad off is Andrew Johnson?" *Please say he's going to be okay.*

Looking nervous, she replies, "I'm sorry. I'm unable to go into specifics with you about another patient. It's part of our privacy policy."

"So he *is* a patient then?"

She bounces from one foot to another. "I can't say if he is or isn't, and won't disclose names *but* ..." She pauses, as a crease forms between her brows. "From what I've heard, *you* are the only survivor amongst the group of you who came in together. The second survivor passed away earlier today," she adds sympathetically.

"No, no, no. That can't be right. There were several of us. Andrew's in his late forties, 'bout my size, got a bushy, gray beard. You can't miss him," I say, gesturing with my fingers.

"I'm sorry." There's pity in her features. "He was the other survivor. We just lost him today."

Bile slides up my throat, and I'm suddenly looking for something to throw up in. "I need a bucket," I say, glancing at Lauren. "Somebody get me a fucking bucket!"

Julie scurries to the bathroom, rushing back with a trashcan in her hand. I grab it and hurl into it three times. Every part of me hurts. Lauren tries to soothe me, but I want to be left alone, knowing I'm responsible for this. I killed him by bringing him into my world, and Reese will never be able to forgive me for it.

Lying back against the pillow, unable to look anyone in the face, I mutter, "I need some time." Swallowing down the pain, I continue, "Nothing against you, Lauren. Just give me an hour."

"Okay." Her voice is shaky. "I'll give you some time. I love you, big brother. And I'm proud of you."

I choke, staring at the wall where no one can see the guilt

consuming me. "I love you, too."

I've been staring at the ceiling for twenty minutes, wishing there was a way I could turn back the clock and not handle things the way I had that night. I was a second too late—one second. I should have never turned my back on my father. Why did I start with Marcus? Why? Glenn has always been the real villain. Two people died that night because of me.

"How are you feeling, sweetie?" The nurse comes in and checks on my vitals.

"You don't want me to answer that."

She considers me a moment, her eyes showing pity. "Our chaplain is right outside your door. He was wondering if he could have a word with you?"

"Send him in," I tell her, glancing in that direction.

She peeks around the corner, and they exchange a few words before the chaplain walks in.

"Hello Luke." He smiles. "I'm Pastor Sorenson, one of the chaplains here at the hospital. I understand you're having a difficult time with some recent events in your life." His voice is filled with concern.

Watching him warily, I mutter, "Uh huh." I'm not sure what all he knows. I don't like the idea of dishing out my personal business.

"I'm also a licensed counselor with the FBI and wondered if you'd like me to pray with you? Many times prayer will help relieve some of the emotional stress one is feeling … sometimes even physical pain."

"That's very kind of you, but I'm going to decline. Thank you, though."

Disappointment flashes across his features, then he nods, digging into his pocket. "Here's my card if you change your mind. I've been told I'm a good listener."

I take it and set it on the table, as he starts for the door. "Goodbye, Luke. Remember, you're not alone."

*Where have I heard that before? Andrew.* "You remind me of someone," I blurt out, but he doesn't hear me. He's already gone.

I press the red button to get the nurse's attention. It takes a couple minutes before she prances in with a wide smile and her hands on her hips. "What can I get for you, handsome?"

"I need to make some calls, and there's no phone in here."

Her face falls. "*Unfortunately* …" She sighs. "That I can't help you with. It sounds silly, but the nursing staff was given special orders not to give you a phone, or allow visitors unless they're family. If you're looking for your wife, she'll be here shortly."

*Right.* "You mean Rachelle?"

"Yes, your wife. I called to let her know you're awake. She's thrilled and said she's on her way."

I hold back a groan. "Thanks. Do you know when I'll be allowed to communicate with people outside of the hospital?" I assume the restriction has to do with the investigation. "There are people I need to get ahold of, and it's important." Reese is going to need someone right now, and I want to be there for her.

"I'm sorry, I don't have the answer to that. I'm just following orders, but if anything changes, you'll be the first to know."

Nodding, I tell her, "I appreciate it. Thanks Julie."

Lauren enters the room hesitantly.

I wave her over, feeling bad for kicking her out in the first place "Come in." She drove a long way to see me, and I miss having her around.

Her heels clank against the floor as she prances over and plants another kiss on my cheek. "I'm worried about you, bro."

I pull back and give her a funny look. "What's with all the kissing?" With my good arm, I take a swipe at my cheek.

"Don't be immature. You're my brother," she murmurs, annoyed.

"You never used to do it. It feels weird."

"Well, it's never too late to start. I thought I might have lost you," she says, her brows pinching together. She grabs the chair behind her and scoots it up to the bed. "Are you going to tell me what happened?"

I still haven't told her about Glenn, and I'm not sure how she's going to take it. They've never been close, but he's still her biological father.

"What do you want to know?" I ask, scanning her face, hoping she isn't going to hate me for this.

"The truth." She looks me over. "Did Dad do this?" she asks, her eyes filling with unshed tears. "'Cause it wouldn't surprise me if he did."

"It wasn't him," I tell her.

She inhales a breath. "It wasn't?"

"No," I say, shaking my head. "He was already gone by then."

Relief spreads over her features, then her gaze falls to the ground. "I really thought it was him." She sniffs.

Taking her hand in mine, I look into her eyes. "I killed him, Lauren. I shot him …" I pause, swallowing. "Glenn is dead."

Julie stands in the doorway. Both of us turn our heads.

"Sorry to interrupt. Your wife is here to see you."

Of course she chooses to come at the worst possible time. "We're in the middle of something. Can you ask her to wait?"

"It's fine, Luke," Lauren says, squeezing my hand.

Julie points over her shoulder and whispers, "She's right outside the door. She was waiting up at the nurses' station for quite awhile."

Glancing at Lauren, I say, "You don't want to talk about this?" I just told her I killed our father, and she didn't bat an eye.

Leaning in, she says sincerely, "You did what you had to do." Her eyes glisten. "I never really knew him. To be honest, I'm just glad it wasn't you." Flicking her gaze back to the nurse, she adds, "You can send in the wife."

# 23

## Reese

I've been out of my room twice since I got home last night — both times to use the bathroom. I'd asked Gia to kindly turn away any visitors and thank them for their condolences. She came in once to see if I needed anything, but I told her I'd come out when I was ready. I'm not sure when that's going to be, because if I'm not sleeping, then I'm crying.

Over the course of two days I've lost everything. I'd rather feel nothing at all instead of this almost unbearable ache. At least I'd be able to function that way. I have forty-eight hours to plan a funeral with no idea where to start. I don't even have a picture of him. I've flicked through my photos seven times in hopes one would magically appear. Unfortunately, it never occurred to me to take a picture when I had the chance.

I dial his number and press the receiver to my ear. After four rings, the greeting picks up. I listen all the way 'til the end, then hang up, and toss my phone on the bed. I've already left three messages — one telling him that I miss him, the other filling him in on Luke and the wife I didn't know he had. The message was cut off before I could finish, so I called a third time to tell him the rest. I'd love to hear his response to that.

Laughing and crying at the same time, I gaze at the ceiling. My dad didn't know anymore than I had. Luke had fooled us both. The longer I mull it over, the angrier I become. He'd strung me along—played me like an instrument—just like Sean had said, and I was dumb enough to fall for it. I'd come to his defense. I'd thought he loved me. I'd even thought I'd hallucinated that whole scene at the hospital. But then it all started to make sense.

The letter. He had sent it four months ago, telling me to move on—that we *both* should move on. I'd stopped receiving his texts sometime before that. Maybe that was around the time he realized he didn't love me—he had fallen for someone else.

I wonder where they met, and how long they've known each other. Did he fall for her instantly, or is she a part of his past? And where are they living? Is he planning to abandon his home or rent it out like the others? I couldn't bear seeing the two of them together, living happily ever after. No, if that were to happen, I'd move far away from them. No question.

Why had he come here the other day, stringing me along the way that he did? Telling me he loved me? Is it possible to love two people at the same time? It doesn't matter. I wasn't enough. With him, I've never been enough. Why couldn't he just leave it as it was? And the anguish on his face that night—was it the guilt for what he had done to me? I remember he kept apologizing, but he couldn't look me in the face. I'd felt sorry for him and willingly took him in my arms. I nearly *had sex* with him that night.

*Oh my God, he made me an adulteress!*

How can I tell anybody about this? I can't!

"Tell anybody what?" Gia asks, stepping through the doorway. "You don't have to tell anybody anything. I told you that," she adds gently. "I'll tell them for you."

I suck in a breath, unable to give her the truth in this moment.

"Thank you," I reply with a sniffle. It's just too humiliating to bring it up, especially since she'd warned me about him to begin with, and I ignored her advice. She and Logan will eventually find out about my naivety ... from Luke.

"I mean it, Reese," she says, a crease forming between her brows. "Give me your phone. I'll take care it." She holds out her hand, and I give it to her.

"If a man named Thomas calls, I need to talk to him. He may have some answers about my dad." Blowing my nose for the umpteenth time, I climb out of bed and gather up the used tissues to throw them in the garbage.

"Got it," she says, plopping down on my bed, facing me as I stand in the bathroom.

I check my appearance in the mirror. "Ugh. I look like I've been to hell and back." My eyes are red and swollen, and my skin is blotchy. Walking back to my bed, I fall beside my friend. "When does this get easier?" Tears prick the backs of my eyes again. "He's really gone. I have two days to plan a funeral." Now I'm sobbing. "I don't know what I'm doing." Grabbing another tissue, I bring it up to my nose. "Where do I start? My mother hasn't returned my calls ... I'm so alone right now."

Gia brings me into a hug, and now I'm crying on her shoulder. "Listen Reese." Her voice is serious. "I'm here. Okay? We're going to get through this. Together." Pulling away, she makes me look at her. "Do you hear me?" Her brows shoot up, but I'm too busy crying to answer her. So I nod and cover my face.

"I don't know what I'd do without you ... really, I don't," I tell her.

Rubbing circles over my back with her palm, she says, "Lets get you something to eat. And maybe a shower."

Both of us laugh at that.

"By the way, Sean came by to see you. I told him to come back in a couple hours."

After showering and eating a half a bowl of chicken noodle soup, I climbed back into bed—eventually answering one of Pam's calls, before handing my phone back to Gia. I knew she'd been worried about me, and I felt bad leaving her hanging any longer. Like Gia, she offered to help out with the funeral arrangements. I guess I'm not as alone as I thought. And for that, I am thankful.

I hear Sean's voice coming from the hall, followed by footsteps and a knock. "Are you decent?"

I guess that would depend on his definition of decent. I give myself a quick onceover. "You can come in, Sean," I answer, sitting up. Relief washes over me when the door opens and I see him—just now realizing how much I've missed him these past few days.

There's worry all over his expression, as he makes his way to my side of the bed. "Is it okay if I sit?" He hesitates, and looks at me questioningly.

"Of course," I say, patting the space beside me, then I reach out for a hug. He wraps his strong arms around me, and I can smell his Old Spice cologne.

"I'm sorry," he says sincerely, pressing a gentle kiss to the top of my head. "I came by a couple times, but Gia didn't want me to bug you."

"I told her to send away the visitors. I was a mess," I murmur into his chest.

He squeezes me tighter. "I wish I could make it better

somehow." He's scooted us back so we're leaning against the headboard. "I know it hurts."

"Can you stay for awhile?" I ask, licking my lips. "I'll try not to cry. Promise."

Chuckling softly, he replies, "You think crying would chase me away? Really?"

I pull back and look into his eyes. "No. You'd stay."

I barely manage a grin. "You're a good friend, Sean."

"I know."

"I hope I'm not keeping you from your work." He works all the time, and I know it stresses him out when he falls behind. "You could get some things done over here if you need to. I won't bug you."

"Nah, I'm taking the night off. I'm all yours," he tells me, getting comfortable. "Let's just hope the *boyfriend* doesn't get jealous."

My stomach sinks, and I suck in a breath.

His head dips down to meet my gaze. "You're not going to be in trouble if he catches me here, are you?"

*Trouble?* Clearing my throat, I say, "N-No. Not at all." My eyes move in every direction, except toward him. I know he can read me pretty easily.

"Has he been here to see you?" Cocking a brow, he adds, "Check on you? Given you a call? Please tell me he's talked to you," he says angrily, like he already knows the answer.

*Stop! Stop asking questions!* I internally count to ten. "We aren't together anymore," I blurt out. "It's over between us. And please … please don't ask. I don't want to talk about it right now," I say, exasperated.

He stiffens beside me, and we're silent for a few minutes, "*All right*, I won't ask," he finally says, without looking straight at me.

"Can you tell me one thing?"

I close my eyes, clenching my jaw. "I said, don't ask!"

"Okay, sorry … I'll shut up."

"Thank you."

He pauses, seeming to think about his next words. "*So*, what do you want to talk about?" he asks carefully, looking like a puppy who's recently been kicked.

"I'm sorry," I groan. He came here to comfort me, and I go and bite his head off. "You didn't deserve for me to snap at you. Thanks for putting up with my bitchiness," I say, nudging his shoulder. "I'm really glad you're here."

He flashes a dimpled smile then puts an arm around me. "Don't worry. You're forgiven."

## 24

## Luke

"**W**ell look at what the cat dragged in," I grumble, watching Rachelle prance into my hospital room wearing my shirt, with a pair of jeans and some cowgirl boots. "Rachelle, this is Lauren, my sister. Lauren, this is Rachelle, my lawful-wedded *wife*."

"*Yeah*. We've met already … a couple of times," Rachelle replies, like she could care less. "Glad to see you're feeling better," she adds, treading toward my bedside.

I pin her with my stare, wondering what she's up to. "Glad you're getting use out of my shirt." *Not really*.

She shrugs. "Thought I'd wear it for good luck. Looks like it worked."

Getting out of her chair, Lauren says, "I'll leave you two alone for a bit." She grabs her purse and tucks her hair behind her ear.

"Stay," I tell her. "Unless you're ready for a break." I don't want her to feel like she has to stay for me.

Clearing her throat, she says, "There *are* a few things I need to discuss with you, in private," Rachelle intercedes, her gaze flicking to Lauren like she's a nuisance. It pisses me off.

"She can stay if she wants." I slowly move my injured leg to get the blood circulating. "I don't keep secrets from her."

Lauren tips her head. "I think I'll go down to the cafeteria. My stomach's been growling. Can I get you anything?"

"*Yesss*. Frozen yogurt, please."

"What flavor." She grins like something is funny.

My gaze moves up to the ceiling, as I think. "How 'bout vanilla, with some chocolate sprinkles if they have it," I add, gesturing with my fingers.

"All right. I *knew* that's what you'd say by the way." She points at me as she's walking out the door.

"Thanks, sis!" I try to yell loud enough so she can hear me.

Rachelle purses her lips. "Cute." Her cheeks are coloring.

"What?"

"Chocolate sprinkles."

I fix my pillow and lay my head back. "I'm treatin' myself. Now, what's the deal with you telling everybody you're my wife?" I cock a brow. "My sister? C'mon, she's family."

"They're only allowing family in here, and I wanted to see how you were. Did she tell you I have your dog?"

"Yeah, she did."

Toying with the corner of my sheet, she lifts it up and takes a peek underneath.

I swat her hand away and flinch in the process, then narrow my eyes at her. "What the hell are you looking for under there?"

"I was checking out your injuries," she snaps with a glare. "Don't flatter yourself." Plopping herself down on the chair, she rests her palms on her knees. "Anyway, your dog's been taken care of."

Blowing out a breath, I relax a bit. "I'll pick him up once I'm out of here. I appreciate it. And thank you," I add, meaning it.

Her eyes light up with a small trace of a grin. "You're

welcome." She gives a single nod then grows silent. "So what exactly happened that night?" she asks finally, tilting her head. "Do you remember?"

Every part of that night flashes through my mind, from Warren standing over my couch, to lying next to Andrew, both of us waiting for death to take us. "I remember all of it, up until I got shot. Next thing I know, I'm in here. Where'd you go after I dropped you off that day?" I can't help but wonder if that's how they found us, if she'd tipped them off.

She sighs. "I told your father I wasn't feeling well … faked the stomach flu. Then I contacted my boss and told him what had happened as soon as I got home."

"And …"

"*And* we were able to track down the person who sent the text," she replies, raising her brows. "It turns out one of the DEA agents working with the FBI was under internal investigation. There were suspicions that he'd gone rogue. He was also the only other person who could have had access to the codes. Once I told my boss everything, it confirmed his suspicions."

"Did you find out why he put the hit on me?"

"He'd been leaking information to both Sergio Valdez and your father. Valdez put the hit on you."

I think about that for a minute. "Why? Why didn't he just do it himself?"

"He wanted you dead, but he didn't want to own up to it." She shrugs. "Continuing a long term business relationship with your father was more important."

Letting out a short laugh, I say, "Glenn wouldn't have cared." I shift in the bed to keep my leg from cramping up.

"Maybe not, but I guess we'll never know." She leans back, and we're silent for a moment.

"How'd Glenn find out about Andrew?" I ask.

"Through the same DEA agent. His name is Devon Hardesty. The guy got around."

"They'd tapped into his phone—found out he was warning Glenn about the set

up. Then they intervened."

"A little late, don't you think?"

She nods. "You're very lucky, by the way. You were the only two to make it out alive."

"Luck has nothing to do with it," I say, tipping my head. "How'd they find us out there?" I groan, lightly rubbing my shoulder, feeling pain as my meds wear off. "Sorry. Go ahead."

"You all right?"

"Yeah, just a little stiff." I gesture for her to continue.

"Warren tipped off the feds."

Now that surprises me. "Warren?"

She's nodding again. "He was an undercover FBI agent."

"Did you know?" I never would have guessed, until maybe that last night I was with him. He seemed different in the way he acted toward me.

"Not until two days ago." She licks her lips. "It's a safety thing. People go rogue all the time. Sadly, it's pretty common," she adds.

"He'd told me, 'Shit is about to go down' that night ... like a warning. He knew we were walking into a gun show," I say, pressing my lips together tightly. "That explains a lot. After I'd been hit a few times, I could still hear the gunfire. I didn't know if I had lost all feeling in my body, or if they had another target," I add, shaking my head. "It's too bad he didn't make it." This makes me think about Andrew again. "Andrew passed away earlier," I say solemnly.

"I heard." She eyes me curiously. "I'm sorry. I wasn't aware that the two of you knew each other before this."

"Like you said, safety reasons." Scrubbing my face with my hands, I'm reminded again. "Can you tell me why the hospital staff was told not to let me use a phone? Am I a criminal?"

"No," she replies quickly. "That's not what it is." Leaning forward to speak quietly, she says, "They have to clear you for *two murders*, Luke. It's proper procedure. After that, you can go back to your normal routine, and pretend like this never happened. This case isn't over yet, especially for you. It's going to take more time." She leans back.

I feel like breaking something. "How much time are we talking about? And how'd you know I killed Glenn?"

Her brows pinch together. "You confessed when they picked you up. You don't remember?"

"Look ..." I stare at her pointedly, sitting up. "There are people I need to talk to. When are they planning to lift this restriction?"

"I told you. When you're cleared," she says like it's obvious. "And when they're positive there are no other hits on you."

"Glenn's dead. Valdez is in prison. I don't understand."

Tilting her head, obviously annoyed with me, she says, "They both had an army of men working under them. It wouldn't be safe to go back to your old life right now. If anybody wanted to find you, they could."

"You're saying I can't go home? Fuck that! I thought this was over." I rake a hand through my hair.

"They'll put you up at a hotel somewhere under a different identification. But it's only until the investigation's complete. It'll be fine."

"Fine for who? What about my girlfriend? I'm stuck in this bed, while she's dealing with her father's murder. She needs me!

Who the hell's going to watch out for her, if I'm shacked up in a hotel?"

She works the details in her head then stands up. "So there *is* a girlfriend." She brings her face close to mine. "You lie," she says, slowly scanning my face.

I stare right back. "I want to know she'll be safe." My jaw clenches tightly. "Is she going to be in danger?"

"Are you willing to stay away from her?" She arches a brow.

"They can't keep me from her. I won't do it."

"Guess she doesn't mean that much to you then." She backs away. "'Cause if you care about this girl, you'll leave her alone until they clear you."

"Luke, is everything okay?" Lauren asks, walking in with my frozen yogurt, clearly noticing the tension. Her eyes flick from me to Rachelle, then she glares at her. "I need to speak with my brother in private now," she spits out, throwing Rachelle's words from earlier back at her.

Rachelle purses her lips, raising her eyebrows at me, like she expects I'm going to defend her.

"She was just leaving."

## 25

## Reese

It's been nearly three weeks since my father passed away, and life is slowly returning to normal. Gia, Pam, and several others helped plan a beautiful ceremony for the funeral. When the service was over, we gathered for a memorial dinner that Pam held in her home. I got to see some familiar faces and listen to stories about my father that I hadn't heard before. As sad as it'd made me to hear them, I'm so happy I did.

I'd finally heard back from my mother a couple of days later. She had taken the news hard, apologizing for not being here. We'd talked for close to an hour, taking turns sobbing while I explained all that had happened in the hospital. At the end of our conversation, she told me she loved me, but she wanted some time to cry alone while Tim wasn't home. We haven't spoken since.

Right after changing into a cotton sleep shirt and comfy shorts, I hear a knock at the front door. Sean and I are watching a movie tonight—probably a horror flick since it's his turn to pick. He owns practically all of them.

I tread down the hallway, past the kitchen and through the living room, finally reaching the door by the second knock.

Swinging it open, I exhale. "Sorry. I was changing." My eyes widen at what I see.

"Hello gorgeous." Sean stands there with a smile, holding a bouquet of pink roses in one hand, a bag of groceries in the other. He's got his hair gelled high, even though it's short. He's wearing a light blue t-shirt and jeans that fit his body nicely. He seems to be in an extra good mood tonight.

"Are those for me?" I grin, reaching for the flowers.

He curiously watches my reaction. "Do you like them?"

"Of course. They're beautiful. I'm just surprised. Thank you," I reply, taking them to the kitchen to put them in some water. "Why did you buy them for me?" I regret the question as soon as it leaves my mouth. I know Sean has feelings for me that go beyond our friendship. He's made no practice of hiding it.

He's right behind me with the groceries, setting them on the counter. "Why not?" He pulls out a couple pints of ice cream. "Cookies 'n' Cream, right? That's your favorite?" he asks, nudging me with it.

"Yeah," I say awkwardly. We've spent a lot of time together the last few weeks, but tonight feels strangely intimate. I'm not sure if I'm ready for that just yet. The pain from Luke is still fresh. It's going to take some time for me to heal completely, and I don't want to hurt Sean in the process. Snapping out of my thoughts, I tell him, "Again thank you. It's very sweet." Maybe I'm making this bigger than it is.

"You're welcome," he answers, scooping out a bowl of ice cream for himself. "By the way, I hope you like *The Notebook* 'cause that's what I brought." Taking a bite, he walks right over to the couch and plops down on it.

"Did something hit you over the head today?" I tilt my head, scooping out my own bowl before scurrying over to the couch, sitting down beside him. "We never watch chick flicks together. Are you feeling okay?" I mockingly place my hand on his head to check for a fever.

With a mouth full of ice cream, he laughs. "I'm feeling fine. I thought I remembered you saying you liked *The Notebook* so I brought it. I actually like the movie."

Biting my bottom lip, I say, "What about the flowers? I've never asked you for flowers."

He shrugs. "So I bought you flowers. You deserve them."

"I do?"

"Yeah, you do," he says seriously, then asks, "What kind's your favorite?" He flashes me a dimpled smile.

"I like the kind you bought me. Roses are beautiful," I tell him, not wanting to hurt his feelings.

He's not buying it. "No. Honestly," he says, shoving another spoonful of ice cream into his mouth. "Tell me the truth."

"Okay fine," I reply. "I love calla lilies. They're my favorite."

"Good to know." He nods. "Thanks for being truthful. I'd rather not waste money buying you something you don't like."

"You don't have to buy me flowers. *Really*, you don't."

"I know I don't *have* to." His brows pinch together as he stares into his bowl. "I want to."

My heart swells from his honesty. If he wants to buy me flowers, how can I stop him? I pause, appraising him for a moment. "Thank you, Sean. You've been such a good friend."

"You've already thanked me three times. Let's start the movie. I got a late night tonight." He lifts his chin. "Still catching up on work."

"Sorry."

Sean didn't make it through the movie. He'd fallen asleep with his head on my shoulder. His small snores were what clued me in, and I felt bad waking him up, but knew he still had some work to do. He fell behind, and I feel partly responsible for it. Now he's ready to head home, and we're standing in the front of the house, enjoying the beautiful weather.

"I talked to Thomas today ... the guy with the FBI," I note, kicking some rocks away from the walkway.

"You did?" He runs a hand over the top of his head.

"Yeah, I'm bugging him, but I don't care."

With his eyebrows quirked, he asks, "Did he tell you anything new?"

I lick my lips. "Just that the investigation is almost complete. Like last time, he reassured me the person who shot my father is deceased. Told me to call him if I had any more questions." I shrug. "I'm sure I'll call him again."

"He was your father. Don't worry about bugging him." He tilts his head, taking a step toward me.

"I'm not." An unexpected breeze passes over us, causing a chill to run through me. I slide my palms up and down my arms, warming myself up.

"Here," Sean says, coming closer and sliding his own hands over my skin. "That better?"

My gaze flicks up to his. "Yes. Thank you."

"That's four." His mouth tips as he stays in the same spot.

"What?" A moment later I grin, realizing it's the fourth time I've thanked him tonight.

"You know what." He chuckles softly, still running his hands over my arms. "I'm going to show you how a woman deserves to be treated. You'll see ..." He narrows his eyes on me. "That Luke guy's a loser. How'd you ever end up with him anyway?"

"Sean, please don't even go there,"

He stops me. "Just hear me out on this. Please."

It's hard to turn him down when he looks serious. "Go ahead," I tell him quietly, hoping he doesn't ask something I'm not ready to answer.

He gazes deeply into my eyes. "I know you're not ready for a relationship right now, and I understand that. But if I want to buy you flowers, let me buy you flowers. Let me take you to places you've never been. Don't you think you deserve that?"

I nod slowly. "No, you're right. I—"

"He abandoned you, Reese. He discarded and abandoned you, but you still love him. It's clear all over your face."

I flick my eyes away from his. "I can't just snap my fingers and turn off my feelings," I reply, unsure what else to say. "I don't know what's wrong with me."

His eyes soften. "There's *nothing* wrong with you. That's what I'm trying to tell you. Can you consider giving us nicer guys a chance? I'll wait until you're ready. You're worth it to me." He sighs, looking up at the sky. "Just tell me if I'm wasting my time here."

I blink once, maybe twice. "No. Believe me, Sean, I've thought about it. I think maybe with time we—"

"Shh." Smiling, he leans down and plants a soft, lingering kiss right on the lower part of my jaw. I hadn't expected it, but it felt nice. "That's all I needed to know," he says, pulling back.

Then I stand in stunned silence and watch him walk away.

# 26
## Luke

**Three Months Later**

"You about ready?" I say to Chance, with a pat on top of his head. We've been living at the Westin in Scottsdale for about three months now, and it's been rough on both of us. After I'd gotten out of the hospital I told them to get me a place that was pet-friendly. There was no way I was leaving my dog with Rachelle for all that time. He'd made that clear when he jumped into my arms, knocking the wind out of me on Rachelle's tiled floor.

After nine additional arrests, and Isabel's sworn testimony, I've received my keys to freedom. If Isabel weren't such a hard woman to track, this investigation would've been wrapped up over a month ago. Turns out, she and her kids were in Mexico with a family friend, trying to start a new life. Starting over there probably made her feel safer.

I did spend a little time with Rachelle. Being holed up in this hotel made her feel sorry for me, so she came by a few times with dinner and played with Chance. He doesn't seem to mind her, and I've learned she isn't as bad as I made her out to be. I was pissed at what she said—that if *I really cared about Reese I'd avoid her*—but in all honesty, she was right. Her safety had to be my priority, so I had to keep away from her.

Chance sits back on his hind legs and watches me.

I stand in front of the mirror one last time, working over the details in my head. I've been dying to see Reese. I miss her and the way her big eyes light up when she looks at me, like I'm her favorite person in the world. I miss the curve of her mouth when she smiles, and the way it turns down when she's frustrated with me. I miss everything that is Reese. I don't want to lose her. How will she ever forgive me? Will she understand? I can't even forgive myself for bringing her father into this mess. Will she look at me the same way? Or will the death of her father be all she's able to see? I never expected things to come to this. And though it's been a few months, I can still barely stand the sight of my own reflection.

I don't know where her heart is at anymore. All I know is I can't stay away from her any longer. I'm ready to go home.

"C'mon boy. Let's go."

# 27

## Reese

This week has gone by in a flash. Tonight, Pam insisted I leave work early to take advantage of having my place to myself. Logan and Gia decided on a camping trip for the weekend, because the weather here is way too hot. I won't have to deal with Logan's dirty looks or snide remarks for a whole two days, which is enough to keep me smiling. I may end up buying a couple gallons of ice cream and plop myself down on the couch all night—watching chick flicks and getting fat.

As I walk toward my house I see several tiny lights twinkling through the window. *That's odd.* Once I'm close enough I get a better peek. A countless number of candles flicker from everywhere inside. I unlock the door and open it, confused. "Hello?" I call out. "Is anybody here?" My eyes fall to the ground. Rose petals in every color line the floor.

I carefully step inside without an answer, hesitating as I walk through the entry. Trying not to crush the colorful petals, it's hard to avoid them; they're everywhere. "Logan?" Would he have planned something for Gia and not told me?

I check my cell phone for missed calls or messages, but there aren't any. "Logan?" I call again, wondering if maybe they changed their minds about leaving. In the back of my brain I think of the possibility that this could be Sean's doing. He's never gone to this extreme, but things have started picking up between us recently.

I'd finally let him kiss me last week. We'd spent the whole day together. He'd walked me to my door, looking nervous like a boy on a first date. Something melted inside me. He'd been so patient with me, but I knew what he was battling with on my doorstep. He didn't want to push me. "*Kiss me*," I'd told him. And that's exactly what he did. It was tender and sweet, but when he pulled away, I was breathless.

He grinned. "That was some kiss," he'd replied, his eyes sparkling.

"Did I just walk into the wrong house?" I glance around, seeing my chair and my couch. This *is* definitely my house. "Hello!"

A small square card rests on top of the counter, my name scrawled on the front of it. Once it registers that all of this is for me, my nerves start to consume me. I'm excited and scared at the same time. After reaching for the card, I tear it open.

In bold, it reads:


**Dinner on the rooftop, 8:00.**
**Wear the dress.**


Placing the card against my chest, I think, *what dress?* Confused, I make my way into my room, where a large rectangular box with a red ribbon tied around it is lying on top of my bed. I debate on whether to open it, thinking this is all too much, then again, it makes him happy to do these kinds of things for me. So of course I'm going to open it. I pull off the lid.

A crimson-colored fabric lies inside, a halter-style dress with the back cut out, designed to accentuate my curves. *Wow.*

Carrying it into the bathroom, I try it on in front of the mirror, turning from front to back. It looks as if it was tailored to fit my body. To say I'm impressed would be an understatement. It's the perfect mixture of classy and sexy. "Looks like Mr. Lawyer has been doing his homework."

I turn on the shower, then carefully slip out of the dress and hang it up in my closet. Taking two steps back, I admire it for a minute, when another box on the closet floor captures my attention, this one smaller than the last. When I open it, there's a strappy pair of heels peeking out at me, obviously bought to match the dress. I laugh out loud. *Is this really happening?* Sean must love to shop, which I hadn't known about him.

After lathering my body with soap, I stand under the spray thinking about all that's happened in the last few months. I'd finally told Logan and Gia that Luke and I were over, though I didn't offer any details.

It happened about a month ago. We were all sitting in the family room, and Sean had his hand on my thigh. I hadn't even noticed it there until Logan went off on him, saying something like, *"I suggest you find another place for your hand. Don't forget who she belongs to."* Needless to say, I was mortified. After I snapped and told him it was over, he seemed to shut up about it.

When Gia asked about it later I told her it was too exhausting to explain, and honestly, it didn't' matter anymore. She responded with a sad look in her eyes and pulled me into a hug. She hasn't brought it up since. She knows it's bad, but she doesn't know *how bad* it really is.

Rinsing all the soap off my body, I turn off the water and wrap myself in a towel. I only have thirty minutes to get ready, and the butterflies continue to build with every second. I put on my dress and turn on some music for a distraction. My mind is spinning with thoughts of what might happen later.

Finishing my make-up, I apply a light stroke of gloss along my full lips before stepping into my strappy heels. I blow out a breath and glance over my outfit one last time, pleased with what I see. When I check the clock, it's time to go. Excitement fills me, and I flick off the light—stepping on layers of petals as I make my way out. I grab a bottle of my favorite cabernet out of the kitchen, then make my way out the door.

As I reach the top of the stairs, my mouth nearly drops to the cement. The view is stunning. I can't believe the work he put into this. Candles line the perimeter of the entire patio, and there's a table set for two in the middle, covered in dishes of lasagna, salad, and bread. A single, white calla lily rests on one of the plates. I pull out the chair that sits in front of it, setting the bottle of wine in the center.

"Sean," I gasp, as I hear footsteps approaching. "This is incredible." My breath catches when I lift my gaze. "Wh-what are you doing here?" I choke, barely able to speak. "I … I thought you were—" I hold my hand over my chest, my eyes widening. My heart is thumping to the point where it probably isn't safe.

"Sean," Luke answers for me, frustration in his eyes. He's wearing a black tux—the jacket unbuttoned—with a bow tie. He's far too handsome and shouldn't be this close to me. I want to ask him where his wife is and why he's here.

"You did all this?" I ask, gesturing around the patio.

"Yes." He nods, his gaze piercing into mine before almost completely closing the distance between us. I swallow back my tears. Why would he do this? And why does he still have this power over me? He looks like he's hurting, which makes me want to comfort him, and it's so very, very wrong. He's a liar and a cheater, and I'm moving on with Sean.

I lift my chin. "Are you just going to sit there and stare at me all night? What's the point of this?"

He flinches. "I came here for you. And yeah, I'm going to stare at you. Besides the fact that you're the most beautiful woman I've ever seen, I don't want to take my eyes off you because it's been months since I've been able to look at you."

Scooting out of my chair, before I burst into tears, I say, "You shouldn't say things like that to me." I stand up, and he does the same. "Sit down." I back away. "I don't want to be close to you."

"Why are you running from me?" Taking off his jacket, he tosses it over the chair and comes toward me.

"You know why." I hold out my hands and take two steps back.

His brows pinch together. "What's wrong with you? Why aren't you letting me touch you?" He rolls up his sleeves to the elbows, then loosens his collar. He's stressed.

I watch him work his jaw with every single step. "Back up, Luke. I know everything!" I'm shaking in anger, and my eyes well up with tears.

There's determination on his face, as he continues moving toward me until the back of my shoe hits the wall, and his hands are on my shoulders.

An instant jolt of electricity shoots through my body, then he asks angrily, "Is it the neighbor?"

I glare. "How dare you ask me that! You don't have that right anymore."

He leans his head down, and I'm immediately intoxicated by his scent. His mouth is dangerously close to mine. "Talk to me Reese," he whispers, scanning my face like he really does love me.

I shake my head, and try to swallow the lump in my throat. "I don't trust you."

Hurt flashes in his eyes, but I won't fall for it this time. I can't.

"Stop looking at me like—"

"Like what?" he snaps, raking a hand through his hair. "Like it's taking every part of me not to touch you?" he adds, confused. "I just want to be with you."

"You're a liar!" The dam has burst, and now I'm sobbing. "I lost my father three months ago. I was alone!"

"I should have been there for you, and I'm *so* sorry I wasn't."

I wipe my face with the back of my hands. "I don't want to hear your excuses. I already know the truth."

Surprise flashes over his features.

"That's right, Luke. *I know.*"

His eyes narrow as he watches me for a minute, and then his face pales. "Who told you?"

"Is that all you care about?" *I can't believe that's his response!*

"C'mon." He frowns. "You know me better than that. Look, you have every reason to hate me. But I was protecting you. I couldn't tell you at the time."

"So that makes it okay to go behind my back?"

Nodding, he says, "Yes, in a way. If you'll let me get a word in, I'll explain."

"If you have a heart, you'll spare me the details," I cry. "How could you do this to me?" I'm definitely not holding back.

He tugs at his hair. "I thought that after I told you everything, it would make sense to you why I did it."

"And you thought I'd be okay with it? That I'd just move on and pretend like it never happened? What kind of person do you think I am?" I shove him, but he grabs my wrists and pulls me toward him.

"I'm sorry, Reese ..." He swallows. "I'm hoping one day you can forgive me. I didn't mean for it to happen." A tear rolls down his cheek. I can't believe he's just as upset as I am.

"Get away from me!" I shove him again. "I'll never be able to forgive you!"

His face is full of conflict. "In time you could try." He reaches out to wipe away my tears.

"I said get away from me!" I cry.

He rubs the space between his brows, and his other hand rests on his hip. "You really want to do this? After all the history between us?"

Unable to look at his pain-stricken face, I turn away. "Please. Just leave." I squeeze my eyes shut.

I feel him hesitating behind me, but after a few seconds, his footsteps slowly fade.

I know he's still there, but it's quiet for a moment before he eventually speaks. "I'll respect your wishes and leave you alone, but I'm not going to stop loving you." He gives a sardonic laugh. "I never could."

*The End.*

Stay tuned for the conclusion of Luke and Reese's story in the final book of The Bad Boy Reformed Trilogy, **BREAKING RYANN**.

# Acknowledgments

First of all, I have to thank God for giving me a patient loving husband, healthy beautiful children, a fantastic family and wonderful friends. I want to thank Camryn Pinner once again for the days and hours you spent, reading through my mistakes and encouraging me through the writing process. You totally rock! To my children for being awesome, allowing me to slave away in the den while you were starved and neglected. To my husband who really stepped it up and took care of them during this whole process. I noticed how much you'd helped, and appreciated it immensely. To my loyal fans from Wattpad, who fell in love with Luke Ryann from the first, page. *You know who you are.* I couldn't have pushed forward without al your supportive comments. They mean a lot to me. To Victoria Ashley for her talent as a writer, but for offering her support. To the talented Madison Seidler, for working you're a** off cleaning up the story. Your comments made me laugh and 'cock a brow.' I'm sticking with you. Thank you Sarah Hansen for designing the hot cover. Once again I love your work. Also, I'd like to send a big thanks to EM Tippetts for making my book look pretty within the time crunch that we had. Thank you Kim Person for organizing my last blog tour with Raising Ryann. You did an amazing job and I was surprised by the huge response. Thank you to all the bloggers who participated in helping in its success. To Debra and all those participating in this tour, thank you for giving the series a chance. I hope you all enjoy it. Last but not least, I want to thank all the bloggers who have shared my stories. Without you, I wouldn't have anyone to share them with. Thank you for spreading the word. It's appreciated. Thank you to *all* of my readers!

# About the Author

Wife. Mother. Writer. Reader. Dreamer.

For more information on Alyssa Rae Taylor and her up and coming projects, you can visit her here:

https://www.facebook.com/authoralyssaraetaylor
https://www.goodreads.com/alyssaraetaylor
https://twitter.com/Alyssartaylor
https://www.alyssaraetaylor.com

This paperback interior was designed and formatted by

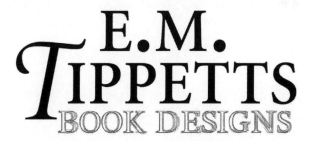

E.M.
TIPPETTS
BOOK DESIGNS

www.emtippettsbookdesigns.com

*Artisan interiors for discerning authors and publishers.*

Printed in Great Britain
by Amazon.co.uk, Ltd.,
Marston Gate.